HUNTER

THE MIXOLOGY SERIES BOOK 1

KRISSY V

For all the Tom Cruise in Cocktail fans out there.

I am trashed. Totally and utterly fucked. I need to stop drinking as I can't really see much of what is going on around me. My bed is beckoning me. Stumbling around the lounge, I look for Grace, but I can't see her. She must be waiting for me upstairs.

There are bodies everywhere. Some of them have passed out and I know I will find them in the same place tomorrow when I'm eventually able to climb out of bed. I love University parties. They're crazy fun. Everyone gets absolutely trollied and has a fantastic time. No one cares what state they're going to be in the next day. College life is living the dream.

Staggering up to my room, I see some more people laid on the stairs, kissing each other. I think I just saw a couple who were attempting to have sex on the stairs. Looks interesting; I might have to suggest that to Grace one night when we're on our own.

Finding my bedroom, I grab hold of the door handle and open the door with a flourish, expecting to see Grace in bed waiting for me. What I see, however, is Grace in bed, but not waiting for me. She is laid on top of the bed naked and she's trying to undress another guy and drag him down on top of her.

I see RED. My head starts throbbing, my eyes glaze over and I can feel my heartbeat pulsing in my ears. I just want to punch whoever the fuck is leaning over Grace right now.

"What the fuck is going on here? Grace, what are you doing? I don't fucking believe you." I stumble into the room, feeling a lot more sober than when I opened the door.

Grabbing the guy who is standing by the bed, I yank him around to face me.

When I see who it is, I almost collapse on the floor.

"What the fuck, Coop?" I shout in his face.

"This is not what it seems like, Hunter. You have seriously got the wrong end of the stick."

"Are you fucking kidding me? You're meant to be my best friend and that is *my* girlfriend, not yours." I swing for him and knock him flat on the ground. Then I jump on top of him and keep punching him. I don't want to stop until he is dead. I'm angry, hurt and feel so let down. Coop and I have been friends for years. We were so happy when we got our results at school and realised that could go to the same University. It just made the whole University experience so much better.

Eventually someone hears the commotion and comes into my bedroom and drags me off him.

"Get the fuck out of here! Get out of my life and take that piece of trash with you." I shout, pointing at Grace. "I don't want to see either of you ever again. I don't even know who you are anymore and I don't fucking care. You mean nothing to me, neither of you."

He leaves the room and Grace tries to make me look at her. "Hunter, I love you! I don't know what happened. I was laid on the bed waiting for you and he came in and started touching me. I didn't do anything, I promise."

"Get the fuck out, Grace. I don't share and I *never* take sloppy seconds. I can't believe you

3

betrayed me like this. I NEVER want to see you again. Fuck off!"

Dragging her out of the bed, I throw her clothes at her and almost push her out of the room.

Slamming the door behind the two of them, I throw myself down on the bed. If I never see either of them again in my lifetime, it will be too soon.

I swear to myself that I will never get into the position of loving someone and trusting another woman in my life. I intend to stay single and ready to mingle forever. I have my family and don't need anyone else. I'm going to look out for number one from now on. No one will ever be able to hurt me again.

BLOW JOB

1/2oz Baileys, ½ Oz Kahlua, Whipped Cream On Top

I hate my job, I really do. I have to serve cocktails to beautiful women all night. All I want to do is fuck them all night long, but I only get to take one home. Except for that one time....

Anyway, I can't dwell on that night because I need to live in the here and now.

Tonight is the first of our singles nights. Everyone thinks this is done for our customers, but if the customers don't pull anyone then we get to take them home... or the bathroom... or the cellar. You get the picture, right?

So, this is the outline of the night's activities. They come in, register, and get a free signature cocktail. Then they mingle and get more free cocktails. Well, they're not really free as they have to pay a registration fee, but they think they're free and that's what counts.

Tonight's cocktail is actually called a "Blow Job," which is technically a quick shot for most people, but my signature speciality of Bailey's, amaretto, and whipped cream is not one that goes down the hatch very quickly. Actually, the slower the better.

"Are you ready, Hunter?" Eddie asks as I'm wiping down the bar. Eddie is one of the barmen who works in Mixology. He's been here since we opened and was my best mate at school.

"As always, mate!" I smile. The anticipation of all these single women is making me. I can't wait to see who comes through the door. "I have everything in order and ready to go in the cocktail booth. All we need now is the sexy ladies!"

He laughs. "That's all you think of - your cock!"

"Too right, Ed. What else is there to think of?"

He shakes his head. He's married and is no longer my wingman. "What about everlasting love? Feeling protective of someone and not wanting to be apart from them?"

I laugh. "Does that really exist?"

"Yeah. That's how I feel about Cindy. When I

met her, I thought she was a one night stand, but she was like a drug. Now I hate being apart from her," he says, shaking his head.

"That's never gonna happen to me, mate. Not when I've got pussy on tap here." I hold my hands up to show him how much I've got. "No way!"

"Are you two ready?" Ainsley shouts as she stands at the door, ready to open up to the long queue of singletons outside. Ainsley is my sister and she manages Mixology so I can create the cocktails. She can be a little bit of a tyrant, but I love her.

Even though Mixology is my bar, my family makes it. Looking around the place, I see Skylar, my youngest brother, with his laptop, ready to beat out the tunes; Keaton, my closest brother, is manning the main bar with Ed; Zac, the middle brother, is at the door, ready to attack if anyone steps out of line, and Ainsley is staring at me, waiting for my thumbs up.

Smiling at her, I hold my thumbs up so she knows to open the doors and let the customers in.

Two hours later, we already know the night has been a success. The ladies are drunk, the men are prowling, and I've got a pocket full of phone numbers. One lady in particular has caught my attention - Bianca.

"Hey, Bianca," I say, looking at her name badge. When the customers register, they have to wear a name badge to make it easier to talk to each other. "How's your evening? Seen any men that tickle your fancy?" I wiggle my eyebrows at her.

"Yeah, definitely," she says, licking her lips, staring at me.

"How about I give you a Mixology special Blow Job? It's tonight's special cocktail... but with a twist," I say, looking her up and down.

She has long blonde hair, a sexy figure all trussed up in a red patent dress, and I'd safely say she's not a virgin. She looks at me through her lashes and says, "I want one of your special Blow Jobs."

Grinning, I know it will be more than just her who wants one when they see what I have to offer.

"Coming right up, babe." Mixing the shot, I take my top off, to her complete surprise. Her eyes open wider and I hope her legs will open like that for me later.

Climbing up on the bar, Keaton starts cheering

and Ed rolls his eyes. Lying down, I know everyone is watching what is unfolding on the cocktail bar.

"I think I'm going to like this," she says, licking her lips.

"I know you are, but not as much as I am!" I say gruffly.

I put the shot in between my legs as her eyes open wide. She slowly lifts her head from my crotch to my face and her eyes change colour, they become hooded and then they sparkle. She smiles at me and then licks her lips. She wants me.

"Take it, babe. Show me what you're gonna do to me later."

After being lifted on the bar by Keaton, she puts her hands on either side of my thighs and I can feel the heat radiating off them. She then, very slowly, leans down and starts licking the shot.

"Babe, don't spill any on my trousers. The aim is that you get the shot all drunk before lifting the glass up. You've got to suck hard."

She gasps. "I can do that."

I really hope she can.

She leans down again and I can feel her hot mouth wrapped around the glass, touching my now erect cock.

She sucks really hard like she's hoovering it up; it's

really fucking sexy. When she's finished, she takes the glass in her mouth and lifts it up to a cheer from the watching crowd. Sitting up, I take the glass out of her mouth with mine and the bar goes even more mental. There are cheers and wolf whistles, and she blushed.

A wave of lust runs through me.

She wipes the back of her hand across her mouth as she had some cream left over. It's really sexy and I can't wait for her to wipe her mouth like that after I come down her throat.

Jumping back down behind the bar, everyone starts asking me for a Blow Job. I can't deny that it makes me feel good, but I don't do any more specials… that one was just for Bianca.

Feeling her watching me, I turn and face her. "When's your break, Hunter?" Everyone knows my name, so it doesn't surprise me when she uses it.

I smile. "In twenty minutes, Biance. You gonna come with me?"

She nods her head while sucking her finger and drawing it out of her mouth with a loud 'pop'. I can't wait to sink my cock into her mouth so she can 'pop' it like that.

As I serve some more drinks, she waits at the end of the bar for me. There are a lot of gorgeous women in here tonight. Am I stupid just saving myself for one? I look over to Bianca, she smiles, and I know I'm making the right decision.

After twenty minutes, I shout over to Keaton, "I'm going for my break. Be back in …" I look over to Bianca, smile, and then say, "Back in half an hour." Keaton follows my eyes and smiles back at me.

"I'll cover for you. I'm sure there are a couple of ladies who want to see what I have to offer." He walks over towards the cocktail booth. "Right, ladies. Are you ready for some fun, Keaton style?"

They all shout "yeah" and he laughs, turning around to make some shots for the ladies.

Walking over to Bianca, I grab her hand and pull her after me. This is going to be quick and hard. Taking her down the corridor past the toilets, I open the last door on the right. This is an office I use when Ainsley gets on my case about orders, taxes, and shit like that. She follows me in and I close the door and push her up against it.

Her breath catches. "So…" I say. "You like blow jobs then, huh?"

She nods.

"Tell me what you like?" I ask, while my hand is

in her hair and pulling it so she has to look up at me.

"I love blow jobs and I want to give you one now." She starts to slide down the door, but I pull her up again.

"My turn first. It's my break and I'm hungry for your pussy."

She smiles and widens her legs for me. I was right; she opens them freely.

Slowly, I work my way down her body, kissing down her neck then her collarbone. I pull one of her breasts free of her red dress and her nipple stands erect, teasing me. I take it into my mouth and suck it, then I bite it.

"Oh my God, Hunter," she says, running her hands though my hair and pushing me further down her body.

Kneading her breast, I kiss up her inner thigh. Using my other hand, I run it up and under her knickers. Actually, scratch that - her thong. She's wet and ready for me. I reluctantly leave her breast and use both hands to open her legs a little bit wider and then I use my fingers to open her lips. "Please… " she whispers.

I indulge her. I gently push my tongue along the

inside of her lips until I reach her clit, then I start flicking and her body starts to tense under me.

"Relax," I say into her core. Her body relaxes a little bit. I grin. I run one of my fingers along her lips and then slide it inside her pussy.

"God, you're wet."

"I've been wet and ready since I took that drink off your cock," she says in a husky voice that goes straight to my cock.

Pulling my finger out, I thrust two of them back inside and start finger fucking her. She squelches she's that wet. I keep flicking her clit with my tongue and then when I start sucking it, she comes all over my fingers. That was a lot quicker than I thought it would be. I chuckle.

"Oh my God," she says breathlessly.

I suck on her pussy and swallow down her cum. It tastes good; a little salty, but good. When she's come down from her high, I slowly stand and kiss her so she can taste herself.

"My turn," she says, sliding down the wall again. This time I let her.

She reaches out and grabs my belt to undo my zip and my shorts then she reaches in and releases my cock.

I'm proud of my cock, just so you know. It's large, thick, and performs well.

"Hunter, the rumours about you are true. You are huge!"

"Stop talking and start sucking, babe. My break is nearly over."

She licks the end of my cock as there's some pre-cum from when she came. I love the sound of a woman orgasming; it really turns me on. She grabs the base of my cock and slowly swallows it all. She must have been practising with an ice pop or something, because, God, she can deep throat. Not many woman can do it right, but I can feel my cock slide past her tongue and down into her throat.

"God, Bianca. That feels so good." I push her head closer to my body. I hold her head in place, enjoying the sounds of her gulping and then I feel her head pull away so she can breathe. "You're like a real life porn star."

She smiles up at me and then resumes sucking and deep throating until I can't take anymore.

"I'm going to come, so if you don't want to swallow it, you better take it out of your mouth."

She looks up at me, smiles, and then opens her mouth wider. She takes the base of my cock and pushes it all in as far back as she can get it. My balls are touching her lips and she has her head tilted to take me all. I thrust slightly, knowing just that movement alone is going to make me jizz down her beautiful throat.

I pull back one last time and thrust in deep. She gulps and then I come deep in her throat. I hear her gulping again and I try to move backwards to let her breathe, but she digs her nails into my arse and keeps me in place until my cock has emptied everything it has down her throat. Then she pushes me away and I hear the big gasp of air she takes.

I lean down because I can see she's exhausted. "That was the best blow job ever," I say, kissing her lips.

When we stand, she wipes her mouth like I hoped she would. I smile. She adjusts herself and straightens herself out and then I give her a quick kiss on the lips and leave. "I'll see you later," I say, smacking her on the arse. She squeals and then giggles.

Keaton sees me coming back from my break and smiles at me. We high five each other and he says, "I'm off on my break now. I'm getting a bit of what you just got." He nods his head towards a little brunette at the end of the bar who is looking all doe-eyed at him.

I laugh and slap him on the shoulder. "Enjoy, but it won't be as good as my break."

He walks away, hooking his arm through the brunette's, going in the same direction I just came from.

The rest of the night is a huge success, and when it's time to slow things down, Skylar starts playing some slow songs. This is the moment when you see the once single people couple up … at least for tonight.

I see Bianca looking at me and shake my head. I have to work. Even though the singles night is nearly over, we have a lot of cleaning up to do before we can leave. She throws back another couple of shots and I feel a little guilty, but I never said I was available for a relationship. She is purely 'fuck once' material.

Skylar finishes the music and then starts to pack everything away. I see a cute little redhead with a pixie cut, watching him. She looks shy, but he doesn't even notice her. I must mention it to him, because she looks like she's his type.

Ainsley is busy asking everyone to leave and Zac is doing what he does best - intimidating everyone to leave. It's very rare we get any trouble in here,

Once they see him, they don't hang around long enough to cause trouble.

Bianca is hanging around at the bar, waiting for me to finish. Everyone else has left except the brunette Keaton was with earlier. I sidle up to Bianca. "Hey. I have to finish up here, but if you can wait half an hour I'll make it worth your while." I wink at her.

Her face lights up. "Okay. Can I have another Blow Job then?" she asks, looking coy.

I smile and make her one, making sure I put extra cream on it so I can see her wipe her mouth again.

She licks her lips as I hand it to her. She goes to grab it and I slide it back off her.

"Ah, ah, ah," I say. "No hands, babe. No hands."

I walk away, not able to watch her drink it without her hands. There are only so many things my cock can take.

After cleaning up and sorting out the bar for tomorrow night, Keaton says to me, "Man, did you see her suck up her shot? I'd love that around my cock!"

I push him. "Fuck off. She's mine! Well, for

tonight anyway." I laugh. I don't mind sharing. There's never enough women to go round.

After we're finished up, we all leave at the same time. They all go in their own directions, off to do who knows what, but I hook my arm through Bianca's and say, "How do we get to your place?"

I never bring them to my house. She is a random hook up and if she knows where I live then she might turn into a stalker and I don't need that.

When we get to hers and she opens the door, I push her in. I want to get hot and heavy, fuck her, and leave. Pushing her up against the wall, I start kissing her, pushing my tongue inside and pull her hair. She has her hands around my neck, pulling me closer.

"Hunter, we need to make it upstairs." She pulls away and I follow her as she runs up the stairs.

When we get into the bedroom, I push her down on the bed and start peeling her red dress off her. She has a fantastic figure and I can't wait to fuck her and watch her tits bounce up and down. They're so fake; I bet she can't even feel me touching them.

She lays on the bed naked and I take off my top and then my jeans. I'm commando, so I'm ready to go at any time. I kiss her body and take my time working my way down her. I can't wait too long; I need to be inside her. I touch her to make sure she's wet enough to take me.

"Bianca, I'm going to fuck you hard. I'm so horny and I need to come."

"Hunter, I want you so bad. Just fuck me."

I take a condom out of my back pocket, rip the packet, and cover my cock in plastic.

"Are you sure you're ready? This is going to be hard and fast."

She nods. I lean over her and kiss her again, letting my tongue slide into her mouth at the same time my cock pushes into her pussy.

"Oh my God." She moans into my mouth.

I hold still to let her get used to my size and then I ram myself fully in. She's wet and hot, but not very tight. Good job I'm big and can still feel her walls as she squeezes them around me. I don't really like the missionary position, it's quite boring, so I pull out and drag her down the bed. She smiles at me. "Hunter, what are you doing?"

"I'm changing it up, babe." I lift her up and she wraps her legs around my waist. I kiss her whilst moving her backwards until she's up against the wall. I slam into her and she climbs up my body and grabs the back of my head.

"Fuck, Hunter!"

"I know, babe. That's what I'm doing!" I keep slamming into her, and she keeps bearing down on me, meeting me stroke for stroke. She feels tighter in this position and she keeps squeezing me, sucking me in.

She starts to unravel around me. "Hunter... oh my God. I'm going to come." She squeezes me tight for the last time and then I push in as far as I can go. "Aargh!"

I lean in and rest my head against hers; we're both breathing heavily.

When I feel my heart rate starting to get back to normal, I slowly pull out of her and move her legs so that she's standing on the floor. "Can you stand on your own?"

"I... I think so." She takes the weight herself and then giggles. "I feel like Bambi."

I laugh. Taking a step back, I take the condom off and tie a knot in it. Looking around for a bathroom, she points to a door in the corner. Going inside, I throw it in the bin. I lean on the counter and look into the mirror. Sweat is pouring down my face, but I still look good.

When I walk back into the bedroom, she's in bed with the duvet folded back for me to get in too. Fuck. This is when it gets awkward. Walking over to my clothes, I start to put my jeans back on.

"Where are you going?" she asks pitifully.

"I'm not staying. I have to get home. I have some stuff to do before I go to sleep. I had a great time. Thanks, Bianca." I walk over, and leaning over her, I kiss her deep and hard. "See you again," I say, and walk out of the bedroom and her house.

I know I'm a bastard, but all she was is someone I hooked up with. I never asked for anything more and I never insinuated anything more.

Walking home, it's a nice night; warm and the moon is shining with not a cloud in the sky, guiding me home.

Walking along the promenade, I see a couple making out in the deck chairs. I know it sounds impossible, but believe me, it's quite fun.

I feel like a stalker, but the woman isn't making nice noises. It sounds like he's forcing her to kiss him. I sit in one of the deck chairs just on the other side of a small wall. They can't hear me.

"Get off me," I hear her mumble as he grinds his mouth over hers.

"You know you want me to, Scarlett. You've been teasing me for long enough. Come on, baby… please," the guy says.

I can't listen to anymore. He needs to respect that when a woman says no, she means no. Even though I'm a player, I'd never force a woman to let me fuck her. I don't need to.

Standing I walk around to the other side of the wall and when I am in front of them I say, "Scarlett, are you okay?"

They both look at me. She nods.

He says, "Who the fuck are you? How do you know my girlfriend?"

He lets her go and starts to stand up, but she grabs his arm. "Finn, leave it alone. I don't know him."

He shrugs out of her grasp.

"She doesn't know who I am, but she doesn't want you to push her either." I stand tall in front of him. He is a good few inches shorter than me and much, much leaner.

"Why do you think you can stick your nose in my business?" He stands on his toes so he can shout into my face.

I push him away slightly. "I don't know your girlfriend, but she said she didn't want to do whatever you were trying to make her do. Leave her alone."

She grabs his arm. "Come on, Finn. Leave it." She steps back into the beam of light from the street light behind the wall and I see her fully for the first time.

She is stunning. I catch my breath. Wow. I've seen a lot of extremely beautiful women in my time, but she makes them all pale into the background. The moonlight is shining on her beautiful honey-coloured hair like a halo, and she has curves in all the right places. She looks at me, smiles, and then looks away. She likes what she sees too.

After what happened to me at Uni I would never take another man's woman. I reach out and touch her to ask if she's happy to stay with him and I feel something I've never felt before. A shock runs through my body like I've met my other half, the missing part of me, the part that will make me whole. I shake my head and take my hand off her.

"Erm... Scarlett, are you going to be okay here?"

She jumps back slightly and just stares at me. I wonder if she felt it too? She looks shocked.

"Erm… yeah. I'll be fine. Thank you." She smiles at me again.

I turn and walk away. It's really the last thing I want to do. I just want to knock him out and run away with her. I don't have these feelings; I must be drunk, although I know I haven't had many drinks tonight.

I hear Finn shout, "Fuck off, you nosy bastard. Come on, Scarlett. We can finish this at home."

I don't turn back around because it's really none of my business.

While walking through Royal Terrace Gardens - which used to be called Rock Walk when I was younger - to get home, I can't stop thinking about Scarlett and how I reacted to her touch. Stopping halfway up the steep steps, I turn and watch them walk away from the gardens towards the old harbour. She looks like she is putting up a bit of fight, but it's none of my business. I only turn and carry on up the hill when I can't see her anymore.

Taking the lift, which brings me straight into my penthouse apartment, I do what I always do when I get home from work. I go straight through the lounge and out onto my wraparound balcony. I just love looking at the bay at night. It's pitch black, but all the fairy lights brighten up the sky with their multicolours twinkling along the bay.

I breathe in the sea air and wonder why I ever left this town. I think I was getting smothered by the whole tourist thing going on, but since I've been back, I realise how beautiful my hometown is. After a few minutes, I walk back inside and go to bed. Fucking Bianca has worn me out.

COCKSUCKING COWBOY

2/3 Oz Irish Cream & 1/3 Oz Butterscotch Schnapps

I slept well after my walk home last night. Fucking always makes me sleep better. Who needs sleeping tablets? All I need is a willing woman I say laughing to myself. I always manage to find at least one.

Stretching, I run my hand down my body over my ripped abs towards the "v" the ladies all love so much. Looking from my viewpoint, it's like an arrow pointing the way to my cock. Talking of which, my hand reaches down and wraps around my rock hard cock. Waking up with a hard-on sucks balls, but I just think back to last night and imagine my hand is Bianca's hot, sweet mouth. I fist my cock, getting faster as the adrenaline runs through me.

In five minutes flat, I come all over my abs, but I don't feel relived at all. Nothing beats a wank better than a woman's small soft hand holding my cock tightly and squeezing every last drop of cum.

🍸 🍸 🍸

After having a quick shower and getting dressed, I start cooking a fry up. Just as I'm about to serve it, Ed walks in. "Hey, Hunter. What ya doing?"

"What does it look like I'm doing? What else would I do at this time of day, tosser!" I pull out another plate and put it on the table with a knife and fork for him. Good job I always cook too much food.

Ed laughs. "Timed that right, didn't I?"

"What about Cindy? Is she not giving you food today?" I sit at the table and put the food onto my plate.

"She had to go to work today. I hate when she works; I don't get to see her much. I miss her then, you know what I mean?"

"No, I don't know what you mean. I don't date, remember?"

"Ah, yes. The serial fucker." He laughs. "One day, Hunter. One day!"

"Well, I can tell you it isn't going to be today. Tonight is 'Cock Sucking Cowboy' night and I intend to lasso me a cowgirl to ride my cock!"

Ed chokes on his food and nearly spits it out. "Shit, man. You're fucked up, do you know that?"

"No, I'm just fucking gorgeous and hung like a horse!" I start laughing; I sound like a fucking porn star.

After eating and clearing up, we head to the bar to check off the orders that are due in. Owning a bar doesn't just mean working at night; there is always a lot of work to be done and I know we will be here for a few hours.

After checking in three orders, we take a break and sit outside with a drink, chilling out. I notice a girl stop and look over at us. She looks familiar and I can feel my heartbeat start to rise. Who is she?

"Ed, do you see that girl over there? Don't stare," I say as he turns his head to look straight at her.

"Nah, I've never seen her before. Maybe she's

just a customer. Are you sure you've not fucked her? She's gorgeous."

I shake my head. "No. I think I'd remember her."

He laughs. "I don't know how. You've had so many of the women around here."

She puts her hand above her eyes as a shield from the hot, blinding sun, and then she waves and smiles at me. Instinctively, I wave back then she turns her back on me and walks away. I want to go after her, find out who she is, find out where she knows me from, but then I remember that if she is one of the girls I slept with then I don't want to reacquaint myself with a past conquest.

"Did you just wave at her?" Ed asks, laughing.

"Yeah, she waved at me so it would have been rude to ignore her. Arsehole."

Ed starts laughing.

I finish my drink and look at the time. "Shit, Ed. I have to run. It's Tuesday. We're having family dinner today because Skylar is away at the weekend."

He laughs. "I can't believe you all still go home for dinner."

"Yeah, and actually, we love it. It keeps us grounded and it keeps us tight." I stand and take my glass inside. "Can you lock up and I'll see you tonight?" I throw the keys at him.

"Sure thing. Enjoy!" he says, catching them.

I go home to change and then head out to Mum and Dad's. They don't live too far away so I take the bike. It's a Ducati Diavel and I love riding it along the coastline.

When I arrive, Ainsley is already here. Walking into the house, I shout, "I'm home."

Mum calls out, "We're in the sun room." I walk through the lounge and out into the sun room, where they are already sitting and drinking what looks like prosecco.

"Started the party without me, I see!"

"Your brothers are late, as usual, so we were just relaxing," she says, taking another sip.

"I'm home!" I hear Keaton's voice from the front door, closely followed by Skylar's, "Hey."

We hear the front door close and they walk in, with Zac trailing behind them, looking miserable, as usual. He's been through such a lot, but he won't help himself and he won't let us help him either. He doesn't say a lot, he just gets angry.

Mum stands. "Right then. Dinner is ready. Boys, come help carry, please."

We all stand and follow Mum into the kitchen

to help carry the food into the dining room. Ainsley gets the drinks for everyone, and Dad sits at the head of the table on one side, leaving room for Mum at the other. They're an amazing couple, like the two bookends of the family. We rely on them for everything and they are here for each one of us. When Zac went through hell in London, Mum and Dad raced to get to him, to help him and to be there for him. They looked after him while he was almost zombified and couldn't do anything.

Everyone sits in the same places every week. Ainsley sits next to Dad, I sit next to Mum, Keaton is next to me, and Zac and Skylar are on the other side of the table.

"So... what's been going on with everyone this week? Skylar?" Mum asks.

He looks up like a deer caught in headlights, which makes me laugh. Keaton kicks me under the table and says "Not cool, man!" I give him the evil eye. He smiles and we both look back at Skylar.

"Erm, nothing much really. I'm off to a convention in Birmingham on Sunday." He looks at me. "Remember I booked the day off?"

"I remember." I smile at him.

"There's some really good software coming out

that I want to look at. I'll show you some stuff when I get back. It'll be really cool to have in Mixology."

"Fantastic. Can't wait," I say with sincerity.

"You can come with me if you want."

"Erm, I'll give it a rain check this time, buddy. Maybe next time."

"Okay," he says, reaching out to put food on his plate.

Ainsley goes next. "I've not done much this week. It's been busy down at Mixology so I've kept to myself."

"Sounds boring, darling," Mum says.

"Yeah. I need something to liven up my life a bit."

"Not too much, Ains," Keaton says. We're all very protective over our sister, to her disgust.

She rolls her eyes.

Keaton starts to talk. "I was down in Watergate Bay today surfing and getting ready for the British Surf Championships in a couple of months."

"How was the surf?" I ask him.

"Yeah, it was good, but I need some big waves to test me. I really need to win this one. If not for me, but to get one over on Dakota fucking Ryan." He grits his teeth.

Skylar laughs. "You still up against her? It must

suck balls to keep losing to a *girl*! She's beaten you in the last four competitions. You need to seriously come up with some new moves or she is going to take the championships from you, yet again." Skylar has all the statistics. I'm not sure how he remembers them all, but he is good with figures.

"Fuck off, Sky!" Keaton says, throwing his bread roll at him.

Everyone starts laughing. This is how our dinners go. We are really lucky that we get on so well as a family.

When we've finished dinner, I help take everything into the kitchen then say, "Sorry, guys. Got to run. It's singles week, and you know what tonight is."

"We all know, thanks!" Zac says. He's the grumpy one who doesn't say much except when he's angry and, believe me, that's a lot.

"It's Cock Sucking Cowboy night!" I walk towards the front door. "Yee ha!"

I chuckle on my drive home. It's time to get ready for tonight. Another shot, and hopefully, another woman.

I always like to stand in Mixology on my own and just look around. It's worked out so much better than I ever thought it could. When I was in the Australia, I went to a lot of cocktail bars to see what I liked and what I didn't like, and when I came home, I put a bit of all of them into my design. There isn't anything in here that I would change. I love my life.

Someone starts rattling the front door. It's Ed, so I open the door and he comes in, chatting about his day. A few minutes later, my siblings follow him in. All of a sudden, there's a lot of chat and my peace and tranquillity has gone.

"Hunter, you never cease to amaze me, mate. Where did you get the fucking cowboy outfit?" Ed says, touching the brim of my Stetson.

"You'll be surprised what I can find in my wardrobe."

Skylar looks at me with his eyes wide and his mouth open. He looks like he wants to say something, but doesn't know how to.

"Sky, I think I need to take you under my wing." I wrap my arm around his shoulder and pull him in close. "Dressing up in the bedroom is so much fun and you're missing out, if you don't do it." I ruffle his hair and leave him standing there staring at me.

KRISSY V

He's far too innocent to be part of our family. I'd even go so far as to guess he's a virgin. I shudder thinking about a James being a virgin in their twenties.

Everyone gets ready for opening, the cocktail booth is ready to go, and Keaton's nod tells me the bar is too. Ainsley looks over at us and we give her the thumbs up and Zac opens the door.

Within twenty minutes, the bar is full, the men and women are mingling, and we have country music playing. Skylar has chosen great music, as usual, and it isn't long before the dance floor is full. The ladies are out doing their line dancing and the guys are standing around watching them.

Scanning the bar, I spy a gorgeous redhead watching me. I smile and she raises her drink and starts to walk towards me. "Hey," I say.

"Watcha, gorgeous. Are you going to give me one of your shots tonight?" she says, and I swear she's resting her tits on the bar.

"Well, that depends." I wink. "What are you looking for?"

She smiles and leans further over the bar. "I'm looking for one night with the Cock Sucking Cowboy." She licks her lips.

I smile back at her. "Well, you never know. You

36

might just be the cowgirl that your cock sucking cowboy needs to ride him tonight!" I pour her a shot and watch as she opens her mouth and pours it down her throat.

Oh, yeah. Tonight is going to be fun.

It's going really well, and we've arranged a floorshow with two cowboys who are shooting each other in a 'high noon' way. They are sexy, buff, and only have brown leather waistcoats over their oiled chests.

Everyone is clapping and each of them has an entourage of women watching them and cheering for them. We don't have to pay them; they just get free drink all night. Oh, and as many women as they can handle.

I notice the redhead is watching me during the show. I sidle over to her and put my arm around her shoulders. "Have you found a cowboy you want to take home tonight?"

"I sure have. What time do you finish?"

I laugh, she is forward I like that. "It's late when I finish, but I'm due a break shortly if you want to get a taste of what's to come." I wink at her.

She smiles. "That sounds great. Just give me the nod, cowboy." She sits on a stool at the bar and I get some more shots ready, slipping her a few along the way to lubricate her mouth for later.

After the show, everyone comes straight to the bar and takes a shot. It's been another successful night.

"Hey, Keaton. I'm taking off for a bit." I nod over to the redhead.

He laughs. "Go get her, cowboy!" He makes a lasso gesture in the air.

I grab the redhead's hand and pull her down the corridor out the back and into my office.

"So, tell me… what's your name?" I ask, just to be polite.

"Clarissa," she whispers.

"Clarissa. I like that. Now, you were telling me you want a ride on this cowboy."

She giggles. "I sure do."

I don't hesitate. I push her against the door and kiss her. She's an okay kisser, but I don't care, I just want to fuck her and move on.

She moans. God, she's making a lot of noise. I run my hands down her body and in between her legs.

"Oh, you're wet for me already. You've been

thinking about this all night, haven't you?" I say, rubbing between her legs.

I don't have time for any preliminaries; I want to be inside her hot, sweet, pussy.

Reaching back, I get a condom out of my pocket and roll it on my big, hard cock. "Are you ready for me?"

"Yeah, I sure am. I want to ride you, cowboy."

I lie down on the rug and turn her away from me. If she wants to ride me then she's going to do a reverse cowboy on me. I don't even need to kiss her or look at her face. All I get to see from that view is her delightful pussy moving up and down my cock, and her fine arse bouncing up and down.

After impaling herself on me, she starts to move slowly.

"Don't go slow, I don't have all night. Fuck me, Clarissa. Ride me hard." If she decides to go slow then I will be grabbing her hips and controlling her movements.

She doesn't disappoint and starts fucking my cock like it's the last thing she's going to do.

"Oh my God, Hunter. Everything they say about you is so true. You are fucking huge."

I laugh to myself. I know the rumours; most of them I started myself just to keep myself amused.

She starts slowing down; she's getting tired. I grab her hips and use her pussy to wank myself off. It doesn't take too long before I feel her orgasm around my cock, squeezing me and taking every drop I have. I follow soon after and slam her down hard when I pulse and cum inside her.

She tries to flop down onto my chest, but because I'm a bastard, I lift her off me and place her down on the floor. I already know I want to move on tonight and not go home with her.

We dress in silence, then when we're ready, I give her a kiss and take her back to the bar. I don't say anything to her for the rest of the night.

It's nearly closing time when I notice a girl watching me. I'm used to women staring at me, but this woman is different. She's beautiful, demurely dressed, and she looks shy. She also looks familiar, but I don't know her. Well, I'm going to change that.

I walk over to where she's sitting with a friend, she's blushing and looking anywhere but at me.

"Hey," she says as I stand next to them.

"Hey. Are you ladies having fun tonight?"

"Erm, yeah. It's not our usual night out, but I was hoping I might bump into you again."

Again? It slowly comes back to me. This is the

girl I talked to last night in the gardens on the promenade and the girl I saw earlier today. What the fuck was her name? How could I forget?

"Well, this is my place, so it's a good place to find me." I smile.

She giggles. "I just wanted to say thank you for last night. Finn was out of order and I dumped him when I got home. Thank you for stopping and checking I was okay. That was really kind of you."

I hunch down so I'm at her level. I want to see her beautiful face. When she turns her head to look directly at me, I can't talk. She's absolutely stunning. How could I forget her?

"I don't like any man to treat a woman like that. You have a right to say no and he should respect that. It sounded like he wasn't going to take your answer either way. Not my place to step in, but I couldn't just walk away."

"Well, I really appreciate it. He was getting really handsy. He wasn't happy that I dumped him, but you made me realise that I don't need to do something I don't want to do."

"Absolutely, and don't ever let anyone do that."

"Scar, are we staying or shall we go?" her friend says.

I look from one to the other. "I'll get you a free

shot if you stay a bit longer. We'll be closing soon, so what's another drink?"

They look at each other and nod their heads. I reluctantly walk away and make them a shot each. When I get to their table, I take out a chair and sit down. "So, I'm Hunter. Who are you two lovely ladies?"

The gorgeous girl smiles. "I'm Scarlett, but you already know that."

Scarlett, of course. I remember thinking of her when I went to bed last night. What a gorgeous name.

"I'm Erin," her friend says, and it takes all my willpower to turn my head and smile at her. It means leaving Scarlett's beautiful face, but somehow I manage.

"I don't think I've see you girls in here before. Are you on holiday or something?" I look from one to the other.

Scarlett blushes. "No, we live here, but this is our first time in here." She looks around and I follow her eyes and see what she's looking at. There are couples kissing and making out all over the place. "It's not really our style, to be honest."

It's like I'm looking at it with fresh eyes. It makes the place look tacky, which is not what I want from Mixology. It's supposed to be high class and stylish, not a dive.

I look at her. "Really? And why is that?"

Erin speaks first, "We don't do random hook-ups and this place is known for them."

Random hook-ups. They're the ones I love the most.

Scarlett is looking at me. She takes her bottom lip into her mouth and bites it. God, my cock is instantly hard. She really is something else and out of my league for sure.

"It's not that we don't hook-up," she says, still staring at me. "It's just that we don't have to get drunk and parade ourselves to get them."

I think she likes me. They've warned me that they don't do random though.

"Scarlett!" Erin shouts at her.

They seem to be saying things to each other purely by the look in their eyes. Scarlett blushes.

Okay, this chick is making me as hard as a fucking rock. I either need to hit on her or move on because I need to ease the pain in my trousers.

"I've got to go and finish up. If you girls want to stay for a lock in, just keep sitting there. I'll make sure Zac doesn't kick you out."

They nod their heads as I walk away. I hope

they stay. I really want to get to know Scarlett a bit better, but I don't think they will. They're not that type.

After about ten minutes, I see them arguing and then they both get up and leave. As they're heading out the door, Scarlett turns and smiles at me, then she raises her hand and gives me a little wave. She looks vulnerable and I want to take her in my arms and hold her tight. Where the fuck did that thought come from? I wave back at her. She blushes then leaves.

"What the fuck? Were you waving at that chick?" Keaton asks, laughing his head off.

"Fuck off. She waved first."

"She is so far out of your league, Hunter. She doesn't do random, you can just tell. She is relationship material if I ever saw it, and we all know you don't do relationships." He slaps me on the shoulder and walks off.

He's right. I don't do relationships. I tried that once when I was in University, and boy, did that backfire on me.

3

SLIPPERY NIPPLE

1/2oz Sambuca, ½ Oz Baileys, Grenadine

G roaning, I roll over in the bed. My head really hurts. That might have something to do with the lock in we had last night. There was just us James' there, but we sure know how to party. It was after four when we locked the doors and made our way home. It was another successful night. This singles week has really taken off and I saw a lot of people making out and leaving together.

Zac only stayed for one drink after closing and clear up. I have to admit, I'm worried about him. He used to be so much fun and then he went to London and earned a fortune, but he came back a broken man. He's never been the same since Erika. I remember going to London, and what I found was not Zac. He wasn't the brother I loved. He is coming around slowly, but he's still a very angry man, which is why he makes the best doorman in town, although we do have to sometimes stop him from going too far and losing his license.

Climbing out of bed slowly, I sit on the edge of the bed for a few minutes to get my equilibrium back. It's a gorgeous day and I walk straight out onto my balcony to see what's going on. It's lunchtime already as I've slept late, as usual. There are a few people on the beach, some surfers, and I wonder if one of them is Keaton. He goes surfing as often as he can. He's training for the next championship somewhere.

I find myself thinking about Scarlett and wonder what she's doing today. Is she working? Does she work? I didn't take her number so I can't find out. That frustrates me no end.

I'm just stretching when my buzzer rings. I wander over and press the button. "Hello."

"Hunter, man. Let me in." It's Ed; he sounds like he's in a hurry. I open the door for him and wait for him to come up in the lift.

As soon as he walks in, he looks like he's been rushing. "What's going on?"

"Have you been to Mixology today?" he asks,

then looks down at me standing with just my boxers on. "I take that as a no."

"Why? What's wrong?"

"Someone tried to break in last night."

"What the fuck?" I go into my bedroom, put on some jeans, and pull a t-shirt over my head. Ed is behind me.

"We have never had a break in in all the years you've had it." Ed says, clearly disturbed. It's like he isn't telling me everything.

"There's more to this, isn't there?" I ask, looking at him while putting my boots on.

"They couldn't get in the back door because of the security system we have, but they made a mess out the back."

I pick up my leather jacket, and as I'm putting it on, I ask, "Like what? Come on, Ed. Spit it out!"

"They left some graffiti that said, 'She's mine!' and smashed up the empty bottles in the yard out the back."

"Fuck!" I storm over to the door and we get into the lift and make our way out to the car park. "Who are they referring to?"

"Who knows, but I'm guessing it's aimed at you. Maybe you messed with the wrong woman the last couple of nights. Maybe one of them was taken or something."

"Listen, I don't ask the girl her relationship status before I fuck her. That's her concern, not mine."

"I knew your whoring around would come and haunt you one day."

I stop and turn around. "Well, you used to do the whoring around too, Ed, and if my memory serves me right, you were worse than me."

He puts his hands up in the air. "Fair point."

I jump on my bike. "See you down there."

Ed appears about five minutes after me, and when I jump off the bike, I immediately see the carnage from last night. I take out my phone and ring Skylar.

"Morning, Hunter," he says when he answers the phone. "What's up?"

"Someone tried to break in last night and when they couldn't get in, they trashed the back. Any chance you can come in and check the security cameras for me? It's your technology that kept them out of the building. Thanks."

"Yeah, no worries. I'll be there in fifteen."

Next I ring Ainsley. She is going to be so pissed.

"Hey, Hunter."

"Ains, can you come down to Mixology? We had an attempted break in last night."

I hear her jump out of bed. "No worries, Hunter. I'll be there in ten minutes."

I know Keaton will be surfing so I don't ring him. I'll chat to him when he's at home.

If I ring Zac, he'll be pissed and will be out looking for whoever did this. But then again, I need him to know who it is so he doesn't let them inside.

"Hunter. What do you want?" Zac says when he answers his phone.

"I need you down at Mixology straight away."

"Okay," he says and then hangs up.

Even though Zac is the one brother who isn't as happy go lucky as the rest of us, he is certainly loyal. He doesn't even know what I need him for, but he will turn up and help out.

It's about half an hour before they're all here and we stand looking around at the mess.

"Fuckers," Ainsley says, then she turns to look at

me. "This is someone who is not happy with you for stealing his girl, at a guess."

"Why the fuck are you blaming me? Keaton has been whoring himself too, you know? And who says it's not Skylar?"

Everyone turns to look at Skylar and we all start laughing. Skylar is the furthest you can get from a whore. I don't even think I've ever seen him with a girl.

"Fuck off, all of you." He turns to look at me. "Do you want my help or not?"

"Of course I do, mate. Sorry."

We take photos and then when we get inside, Skylar goes into the office to check the security cameras. We all huddle around him as he fast forwards and finds the time of the attack.

It looks like it happened only half an hour after we left last night.

"I wonder if they were watching us leave," Zac says.

"It looks like it," Skylar says.

He scrolls through the scene in slow motion so we can see a guy and his mate attempt to break in.

"Can you zoom in on his face so we can see who this fucker is?" Zac asks.

Skylar tries to zoom in, but it's too pixelated. "Does anyone recognise him?"

We scrutinize the picture. To be honest, it could be anyone. I just wish we could get a clearer picture of him and his mate.

"I'll see if I can clean the picture up while you guys clear up the mess," Skylar says.

He starts doing techy things with the computer, so we leave him to it.

"Right," Ainsley says. "Let's clear up. Hunter and Ed, you can scrub the graffiti, and Zac, you can clear the glass up. I'm going to ring the police and get them down here."

"Do we really need to involve the cops? They might start to think we're trouble and we don't need them coming in here every five minutes," I say.

"Right. Okay." She walks inside while we all get organised and start clearing up.

An hour later, it's all clean and there is no trace of damage or graffiti. Skylar comes out of the office to check how we've done and says, "I have tidied it up, but I don't recognise them."

"Come on then. Let's see if any of us recognise them," I say, walking into Mixology.

Skylar does his stuff and then a close up, cleaned up image sits on the screen. We all scrutinize the screen again.

Everyone shakes their heads, but he looks a little familiar to me. I can't place him, but I've definitely seen him before.

"He must be a customer or something. We see so many of them it's hard to remember them all," I say.

"Yeah, that can only be who he is. I'll keep an eye out for him trying to get in. He won't get far," Zac says.

"Yeah, me too," Ainsley adds. "Right, come on. We might as well get ready for opening and then let's get some lunch somewhere."

Even though we cleaned up last night before we left, we still need to restock the bar and get everything ready for tonight. The cocktail/shot tonight is Slippery Nipple and I can't wait to hear all those girls asking for one.

I need to think about my party piece for tonight. Maybe I could let the lucky girl take the shot from my nipple, and if she happens to pull my nipple ring while she's at it, I won't complain.

When we're all getting everything ready, it cuts the time in half, and it's not long before we head to the café next door.

"Ah, the James family. Great to see you all. Take a seat and I'll be over to see what you want," Ivy says.

We don't need menus; we've been here that often. She comes over and takes our order for teas and coffees and then we all order the full hearty breakfast; even Ainsley loves it.

She serves our drinks and then we chat about the Singles Week as we wait.

"So, how do you all think it's gone this week?" I ask.

"I think it's been great. Everyone seems to be having a great time on the dance floor anyway," Skylar says.

"Yeah, the music has been great, Sky," I say.

"Financially, it looks like we've done really well, even with giving away the free drinks," Ainsley says. She's always about the profit and loss. Thank God she is, because I don't care for that kind of thing.

"We haven't had any trouble in the bar, well except for the attempted break in," Zac says, as Ivy puts our plates in front of us.

We're silent when the food comes out. That is one thing us James' are proud of - our love of food.

"So, did you pick up any chicks last night, Hunter?" Skylar asks.

"There was one girl, but it was over quick and I certainly didn't take her home."

"Was that the beautiful girl I saw you with late on?" Ainsley asks.

"No. That's Scarlett. She is beautiful, isn't she? I didn't get her number and I wish I had. I'd love to see her again. I felt a real connection between us."

Zac starts laughing. "The only connection you feel with chicks is your cock in their pussy. You wouldn't know a connection if it slapped you in the face."

"Yes, he does know what one is, Zac. Don't you remember? What was her name? Grace, that's it," Ainsley says.

As soon as Ainsley says her name, I start twitching. It conjures up images I don't want to remember. She betrayed me and so did my best friend. I haven't spoken to either of them since. He did try to contact me, but I didn't let him explain. What was he going to say? "Sorry, dude. My cock slipped into her pussy by accident." Yeah, that wasn't going to wash with me.

"Don't talk about her. I don't want to discuss her or my feelings for her."

"Back off. We were just asking," Zac says.

Breakfast is quiet after that. Ainsley puts her hand over mine and squeezes it to apologise for bringing her name up. I smile at her to say it's okay.

Coming back into Mixology later that evening, we're ready to open the doors and let the singletons in.

The Slippery Nipple shot seems to be a favourite of the lads; maybe they like asking the girls behind the bar for a slippery nipple. Kids, all of them.

It's extra busy tonight. Word must have got around about what a success it's been. I keep looking around, hoping to see Scarlett, but she's not here.

A blonde girl comes up to the bar. She has a really low top on and I can't help but look at her tits. They're standing there, begging for my attention, so I do what any horny man would do. I don't take my eyes off them."

"How can I help you tonight? What are you

drinking?" I ask her, finally dragging my eyes up to her face.

She giggles. "I want one of your famous Slippery Nipples," she says, smiling at me.

"Really? And how do you want it?"

"I'd love to lick it off your own slippery nipple," she replies, blushing.

My cock springs into life.

"I'd prefer to lick if off yours," I say, staring into her beautiful eyes. "Maybe on my break?"

She smiles. "For sure, but for now, will you give me a Hunter special Slippery Nipple?"

I smile and ring the bell. Everyone stops talking and looks towards the bar. They know something is going to happen.

I lean forward and ask, "What's your name?"

"Sophie."

I jump up on the bar. "Sophie here just asked for a Hunter special Slippery Nipple. What do you think? Should I give her one?"

Everyone starts shouting, "Yeah," or "Go for it."

First, I take off my t-shirt, which has all the girls whistling and shouting. Then I take the Slippery Nipple that Keaton hands me and lay down on the bar. Sophie walks closer to the bar and looks at me hesitantly. I'm very muscular; my time in the gym certainly helps with this shot, that's for sure.

"Sophie, I'm going to pour some of this shot in between my pecs and you're going to lick it up. Then I'll pour some more over my nipple. You can lick, suck, bite... whatever you want. Just make sure you get it all up... *wherever* it goes."

She smiles and leans over my chest. I think she's standing on a stool or something so she can reach. Her hands are placed on my chest and she waits for me to pour the drink.

It's freezing when I pour it and it makes my nipples stand to attention immediately.

"Oh my God. Quick, get your hot mouth down there and lick it up," I say, shivering.

She leans in and licks slowly.

"Faster," I shout. It's going to go everywhere otherwise.

She begins to suck it up and then she licks it clean. I hear her groan from the alcohol.

"You ready for the next bit?" I ask.

She nods her head.

"Put your mouth near my nipple and get ready to catch every drop."

I start pouring it and she starts licking, sucking,

and eventually moves her mouth under the small stream of the shot.

My cock is hardening with every lick she makes. I can't help myself. It prods her stomach as she leans over me. She moans and rubs herself over me.

"When's your break, Hunter?" she whispers.

"As soon as you finish licking my nipple!"

She licks as quick as she can, and when she's finished, everyone around the bar cheers. I stand up and jump down on her side of the bar, take her hand, and pull her to the door leading to the office.

"Keaton, I'm out for a while. See you in a bit."

"Sure thing, bro!" he says as he tries to serve all the punters looking for Slippery Nipples.

Y Y Y

When we get into the office, I slam the door shut and slam her up against it. "Fuck. You sure know how to lick your way around my body." I can't remember her name, and to be honest, I don't care. I'm not in this for everlasting love or whatever soppy women call it.

"It was so good." She bites her bottom lip and looks into my eyes. That's me gone. I lean forward and take her bottom lip between my teeth and then

I kiss her. She's not a great kisser, to be honest, but when she pushes her tongue into my mouth, I don't care.

"God, I want you to lick my cock the way you licked my nipples then I want to take your nipples into my mouth and bite them," I say, grinding my cock against her.

"Do it!" she says as she starts to slide down the door until she is eye level with my cock. She unzips my jeans, takes my cock in her hand, and it pops out and puts her sweet lips all over it. I moan when she takes me fully in her mouth; I can feel the back of her throat. I start to thrust and she starts to gag. God, I love that sound.

She is now fucking my cock with her mouth and I love every second of it. I close my eyes and imagine it's Scarlett instead of this girl. The vision of her blonde hair and her blue eyes looking up at me with my cock in her mouth almost sends me over the top.

I take my cock out of her mouth, lift her up, and carry her over to my desk. She squeals, but I don't want her to talk. I want to keep the vision of Scarlett in my mind. I lay her down and pull her knickers down, and after grabbing a condom, I ram myself in to the hilt. There is no stopping me. I'm fucking her hard. But in my mind and my body, I'm not fucking her, I'm fucking Scarlett, and she's driving me mad with desire.

What the fuck is going on with me? Why am I thinking about a girl I haven't even kissed yet? I can have any girl I want; why do I want her more than the others?

"Come on, Hunter. Fuck me hard. Give me everything you've got," the girl beneath me says. She takes the top of her dress down and bunches up her tits so her nipples are taunting me.

Leaning down, I take one of them in my mouth while I squeeze the other one and then I bite down. I ram into her so hard she nearly falls off the other side of the desk. I need this release. I need her. No. I don't. I need Scarlett. I can just picture her beneath me, with those puppy dog eyes and that smile on her face. It's enough to send me flying over the edge and I come with a roar.

"Fuck, Hunter. I thought you were going to push me off the desk you were thrusting so hard," the girl says. What was her name again? I can't remember. I've forgotten her already as I stand there zipping myself up and making sure I'm ready to face the world again.

"Come on. I have to go back to work," I say to

her as she tries to kiss me again. "Maybe later. Let's see how busy I am." I drag her out of the room while she's still pulling her top back up.

I slam the door behind me and someone calls my name. "Hunter?"

Shit. I know whose voice that is. Fuck.

SCARLETT

I promised myself I wouldn't chase Hunter. He's a player. I know he's a player, but, oh my God, he is swoonworthy. After chatting to him last night, I fancied him even more, but I know he's not the right guy for me. I want him though, even if it's just for one night. I think he liked me. He gave me the signs that he did.

Erin didn't want to come with me tonight. She said I'm wasting my time. She told me Hunter goes for the slutty girls and he treats them like slags. She told me I'm too good for him, but what if I don't want to be good anymore? What if I want to be bad for him?

She eventually succumbed and came with me. Well, I offered to pay for her drinks all night and she isn't one to turn down free drink.

When we walk into Mixology, the place is buzzing, as it was last night. They really have a goldmine here.

"What do you want to drink?" Erin asks.

"I think I'm going to try one of those Slippery Nipples. What do you think?"

"Yeah, sure. They're free too. You go find somewhere to sit and I'll get us a couple of drinks."

Erin turns to go to the bar as I look around the place, trying to see if I can find any free tables. There's one in the corner so I walk over, and just as I'm about to sit down, a guy sits in one of the chairs.

"Oy, I'm sitting there," I say.

"Doesn't have your name on it," he says, not moving.

I sit down in the chair beside him and don't say anything.

"So, I guess we're sharing then, are we?" he asks.

"Yep, looks like it." I smile; he's quite good looking, but nothing like Hunter. "It's busy, so why not share?"

When Erin comes over, she smiles when she sees the guy we're sitting with. "Wow, you are a fast mover, Scarlett."

"Scarlett. That's a beautiful name, and please tell me, what is yours?" the guy asks, taking Erin's hand and kissing it.

"I'm Erin, and who the hell are you?"

He chuckles. "I'm Keaton. I'm a barman here and I'm on my break."

"So, you didn't really need to sit down then?" I ask.

"No. I just wanted to meet you. Hunter, was talking about you today and when you walked over to me I thought all my dreams had come true."

"He... he was talking about me?" I blush.

"Oh, yeah! I guess you made quite the impression on him the other night. He's just on his break. He'll be back in a little while. I'll tell him where you are and he can come over and say hi himself."

Keaton stands up. "Ladies, it was a pleasure." And then he walks back to the bar.

"Oh my God, he is gorgeous," Erin says, almost drooling.

"He sure is, but you're safe. I still fancy Hunter more."

We laugh and down our shots. Luckily, Erin has brought two for each of us.

After downing the two shots one after the other, I really need to pee.

"I'm going to the bathroom and I'll get some more drinks on my way back over. See you in a bit," I say as I stand up to walk across the room.

As I pass the bar, Keaton smiles at me, but when he sees me moving towards the bathrooms, he tries to intercept me. "Why don't you stay here and wait for Hunter? He'll be out in a minute."

"I will, but I need to go to the bathroom first. Those two shots have gone straight through me." I smile.

He takes my arm. My eyes shoot up to his and he drops his arm. "Sorry," he says and walks away.

Strange.

I open the door to walk down the corridor to the bathroom, and just as I open the bathroom door, I hear another door open and a girl giggling. Really?

It feels like my whole world is spinning when I turn around and see Hunter walking away from me, dragging a girl behind him who is pulling her top back up. It's very clear what they've been doing. I stand there staring at him.

"Hunter?" I say. I didn't mean to say it. I didn't want him to turn around. I didn't want to make a scene. I wanted the ground to open up and swallow me.

Knowing he's a player and seeing it are two different things. I know it, but I didn't want to see it with my own eyes.

All of a sudden, I feel really stupid. How did I expect to catch the eye of one of the biggest players in Torquay and keep him interested in me?

He turns around and sees me. I think he actually recognised my voice when I said his name.

I don't have any right to be pissed off with him. But I am.

"Scarlett." He drops the other girl's hand. She just stands there, smirking at me. "I looked for you tonight," he says.

I look at her and then back at him. "Really? Well, you didn't look for long, did you?"

I turn to go into the bathroom and he reaches out to grab my arm, before realising it's a bad thing to do, considering how me met.

"Scarlett, don't get pissed off with me. This is me. This is what I do."

I hear the tramp say, "Come on, Hunter. She's not worth it. I'll show you a good time anytime."

"Get the fuck out of here. Don't say that about her. She is worth hundreds of you. Piss off."

He's sticking up for me, but I don't want him to stick up for me to the girl he obviously just fucked.

"Don't worry about it," I say to her. "I'm getting out of here." I push my way into the toilet and slam the door closed. I dive into a cubicle, and when I lock the door, I start to cry.

Have you ever fallen for someone really quickly? You meet them and you know they're going to be important in your life. You fancy them, you know they fancy you, and you can't wait to see them again. Well, that was how I felt about Hunter until five seconds ago. Now, I just want to forget about him and kill him at the same time.

I must have been in the toilet for a good fifteen minutes because I can hear Erin outside the door, looking for me. I wipe my eyes and leave the cubicle.

"What do you mean she's been in there fifteen minutes? Have you been standing out here all that time? What the fuck did you do to her?" She's shouting.

"I just wanted to talk to her. I wanted to tell her how I feel about her. I really like her, Erin, but I don't know how to do the mushy stuff. It's not me. Now she's upset."

"Why is she upset? What did you do?" Erin is like a Rottweiler when she gets started.

"She saw me coming out of the office with another girl."

Erin starts laughing. "You disgust me, do you know that? If you really liked her then you would keep your dick in your pants for at least one night, or more. But Mr Player can't do that, can you?"

"I've never done that. I don't do relationships. Girls know that what they get is one night and that's all."

"Well, Scarlett isn't the right girl for you then. She doesn't do one night stands. She's all in, and there is someone out there who is much better for her than you are. Now move out of the fucking way so I can go and check on my best friend."

I hear a scuffle as he must be moving out of the way. The door opens and Erin walks in, but Hunter is close behind her. He locks the bathroom door after him and just stands there. The tears flow down my face again. He is so gorgeous and I still want him. It doesn't matter for how long, I just want him.

"Erin, I'll be fine. I want to talk to Hunter. I'll be out in a minute." She hugs me. "Honestly, I'll be fine."

Erin looks from Hunter to me and then points her finger at him. "If you make her cry again, I'll fucking kill you myself." She unlocks the door and walks away.

He quickly locks the door again and then slowly makes his way over to me. I step back, and in the process, he has me pinned against the wall.

"Why did it upset you seeing me come out of the office with that girl, Scarlett? Why did you cry?" He has one hand leaning against the wall to the side of my head and one thumb is caressing my cheek. "Why?"

I can't breathe. He is too close to me. He is consuming my soul.

"I... I thought we might had have a connection last night and I wanted to pursue it. But seeing you with that girl just brought home how much of a player you really are. I don't give myself freely like that, so you wouldn't want to be with someone like me."

His thumb stopped caressing my cheek for a while and then he resumes his stroking, but his thumb moves over my lips.

"We do have a connection. It fucking scares me, because I don't do connections. Feelings are for pussies. I fuck and then I leave. That's what I do. But for some reason, I don't want to do that with you and that really frightens me. When I didn't see you tonight, I wanted to prove to myself that I can fuck any girl, leave her, and I wouldn't think about you. Unfortunately for her, all I could see was your face as she sucked my cock."

His dirty talk is making me horny.

"I saw your hair spread all over my desk when I fucked her hard. It was your voice I heard when she screamed my name."

Oh my God. No one has ever spoken to me like that before. The temperature is rising inside me and I can feel the flush appearing on my cheeks.

"When it was over and I could finally see clearly, I knew it wasn't you and I really wanted it to be. I pulled out and told her to get dressed, because she wasn't you." He's moving closer to me.

His thumb is driving me mad and he looks at my lips.

"Hunter…" I say, looking into his eyes.

He leans closer still and then he gently kisses me on my lips. I open my mouth, ready to accept his tongue, but he pulls back.

He rests his forehead on mine and looks into my eyes. "That kiss just proved me right. I want more than a quick fling."

4

SCREAMING ORGASM

1/4oz Vodka, 1/4oz Amaretto, 1/4oz Coffee Liqueur,
1/4oz Irish Cream Liqueur

The sun streaming through the windows bounces on my head and wakes me up. As I stretch in my bed, I recall the events of last night. I see Scarlett's face in my mind and I smile. I hate the fact that I made her cry, but at least it made me realise that I want her. Badly. But I don't want to fuck her and walk away. I want more and I haven't wanted that for so long. It scares me.

Climbing out of bed, I walk out onto my balcony and stand looking at the view. It always calms me down and I like to do my thinking here. All of us James' love the sea, and for those of us who moved away, we've found our way back home, back to the sea. It's so calming and peaceful. You can forget all about your problems and watch the waves crashing into the rocks.

I can't help but think about Scarlett. After I kissed her last night, I took her hand and brought her into the bar with me. Erin and Scarlett sat at a table near the bar and I kept my eye on her. She demands my attention without even realising it. Keaton and I kept them topped up with shots and then we made sure they were both in a taxi before we closed up. Before she left, I took her number and text her before I went to bed. She didn't reply as she was probably asleep. I walk into the kitchen to make coffee and check my phone.

As the coffee is bubbling away in the machine, I lift my phone to check it. I have a reply to my message.

I sent her:

Hunter: Sorry for making you cry. Not sorry because it made me realise how much I care about you.
Scarlett: It's ok. Seeing you with her made me realise how much I care too.
Hunter: Come in tonight and I will make it up to you, I promise.

Scarlett: I don't usually go out to the pub every night of the week you know.
Hunter: I'm sure you don't. Are you willing to make an exception for me? I promise to be good.
Scarlett: I'll think about it.

I don't push her any further. I need to back off and let her make her own mind up. But I hope she does come in; I want to see her again. And soon. It's up to her now, I'll just have to wait and see what happens.

After breakfast, I jump on the bike and head down to Mixology to make sure there hasn't been another attack. There hasn't and everything looks good.

I go inside and start restocking and accepting some deliveries, and before I know it, it's time to go back home for a rest before working tonight. Just as I'm about to leave, Keaton comes in.

"Hey, man. How's things? Just wanted to check up on the place to make sure everything's okay," he says.

"Yeah, it's all good. Have you been surfing all day?" I ask him with a smile.

"Of course. Don't you know it. I have the South

Devon Championships on Sunday and I want to win so badly. The Cornish Championships were last Sunday and Dakota fucking Ryan won, so *when* I win, I will definitely be against her. She is the bane of my fucking life, Hunter." He shakes his head.

"I know. Maybe you just need to fuck her and get it out of your system and then you might appreciate that she's better than you at surfing." I duck before he takes a swing at me. He has a longer arm reach than I have and it's caught me out a few times.

"Fuck off. Yeah, she is good, and I know she's beaten me already a few times, but she is not going to beat me this time. I promise you that." He looks determined and I can well believe that he thinks he's going to beat her, but she is amazing.

"Do you want to grab some food before we rest up for tonight?" Keaton says.

"Great idea. Let's go to the Seaview and grab something quick. I've got a feeling it's going to be a busy night tonight. Thursday nights are the start of the weekend around here." I put my arm around his shoulders and we walk out of the bar.

When we get into the Seaview, we take our usual table and Ivy comes straight over to take our order. We tell her about the graffiti just in case it wasn't someone targeting us. They haven't had any trouble there.

It's nice to sit here with Keaton. I get on with him the best out of my brothers and sister. He's fun-loving like me, whereas Zac is too sensible and angry these days, Skylar is too innocent, and Ainsley is a girl.

"So," he says, smiling. "Tell me about Scarlett." He takes a sip of his coffee.

"There's not much to tell," I say, deliberately being evasive.

"Well, she hung around last night after causing a scene so she must be special. And you didn't take her home last night, so she *definitely* must be special."

"She is special. I haven't felt like this about anyone. You know how I feel about relationships since… Grace." I find it really hard to say her name. She disgusts me and I hate thinking about it.

"I know, but that was years ago. You're not getting any younger," Keaton says, nudging me. "You deserve a bit of regular happiness, not just ten minutes in the office every night."

I ignore him. "Anyway, it's up to her now. It's killing me now knowing if she is coming in or not."

"You invited her down again tonight? You really are a glutton for punishment. What about the women? How are you going to keep them away from their Hunter specials?" He laughs.

I laugh back at him. "I won't be putting the Hunter special on the menu. It's going to be the Keaton special tonight and it should be a good one. Tonight is all about the Screaming Orgasm. The girls are going to go crazy. You just need to think of a good way to sell it!"

"I'm going to enjoy being the special on the board tonight. Get in there!" Keaton says, as he fist pumps the air. There's a twinkle in his eye as he starts to get excited.

For me, this is a momentous occasion. I have passed the James specials onto someone else. It might just be for one night; she might not even come down. I can only dream.

SCARLETT

Sitting at work, all I can think of is Hunter. I know I'm being reckless; he isn't good boyfriend material at all. My last attempt at a boyfriend was a disaster too. Hunter is a player, one of the biggest players in Torquay, but I still want him. Everyone talks about him and his sexual prowess and, of course, I want to sample it and see what they're talking about. I'd be lying if I said it didn't matter; of course it matters. But I felt something with him last night. Even though he had been with that slag, he still cared about my feelings.

Erin thinks he is a big dickhead, but I see him differently. He sets my body on fire just looking at me, and when he was working last night, all I could see was his muscles rippling as he made the drinks. I watched each of the muscles in his face move when he smiled, laughed, or when he was pissed off with someone.

He has captivated me, and it might only be for one night and then he might not want me anymore, but I want that one night with him more than I've wanted *anything* in my life.

I know as soon as I send the text saying I'll think about it that I'll go to Mixology tonight. He's like a drug, drawing me into the abyss of oblivion.

After work, I go home and change, ready to go out. Erin isn't coming with me so I'm going on my own which is epic for me. I'm not the type of girl who goes into a pub on my own, but tonight I am that girl.

I have my black and white bodycon dress on which hugs me in all the right places, and my hair is curly down my back. Add a touch of red lipstick and I'm ready to go. It's nine o'clock, so Mixology has been open for a couple of hours, but I imagine it will still be quiet enough. I take a taxi, and when I get there, I'm surprised there's a queue already to get in.

Standing in the queue, I wait patiently. At the door is a really scary guy and a beautiful woman; I think she's the manager.

"Hi," I say to her when I get to the door. "I'm here to see Hunter." I blush.

She looks me up and down then smiles. "Who isn't, darling?"

I want to run and turn to leave, but I hear my name. When I turn, I see the other good-looking barman. Keaton, I think his name is.

"Yes."

"Come on in. Hunter is going mad waiting to see if you show up or not."

I smile and I can feel the heat starting to burn inside me. He wants me to come in tonight. That makes me so happy.

"Ah, so this is *the* Scarlett," the girl says, looking me up and down again.

The big, scary-looking man laughs. "Is this *the connection*?" he asks Keaton.

"It sure is!" Keaton says, smiling.

"What the hell does that mean?" I ask.

"Hunter told us he felt a *connection* and we laughed at him. But I can see why he would be soft on you," the big guy says. He holds out his hand for me to shake. I do so tentatively. "I'm Zac. Another James brother."

"Another brother?" I shake his hand.

"Yeah. I'm their brother too. Keaton," he says, offering me his hand. I'm just about to move away when the girl speaks as well.

"I'm Ainsley, their sister." She smiles, offering me her hand.

"So it's a family business then? I'm Scarlett, but you all seem to know that."

"That guy in there playing the tunes, that's Skylar. He's our baby brother," Ainsley says.

I smile at them. Wow, the whole family is here

and they all seem to know about me. I'm flattered that Hunter talked about me.

"I'm going to steal her away from you all now. Hunter needs to calm the fuck down because he's like a man possessed in there," he says, pointing to the door. "He's checking the door every five minutes for this beautiful lady." Keaton takes my hand and pulls me into the bar. He doesn't let go until he stands next to a seat and tells me to sit in it.

"Hey, Hunter. Look who I found. She was being harassed by Ainsley and Zac. I rescued her for you," Keaton shouts over to Hunter, who is busy serving shots.

When he turns to look at me, his whole face smiles. It goes all the way to his eyes, and I know I made the right decision coming here tonight.

He walks over to me, leans over the bar, and kisses me on the cheek. "You don't know how happy I am that you came."

"I might have an idea. Keaton told me you were like a bear with a sore head." I laugh.

He turns around to Keaton and swipes him over the top of his head.

They both start laughing. I love the camaraderie they have. I thought they were best friends, not brothers. But now I see they're both.

Hunter walks back over and hands me a shot.

"What's the special tonight?" I ask.

He takes a shot for himself and holds it up for me to clink with his glass.

He looks into my eyes. "This is a Screaming Orgasm. Especially for you." He downs his shot in one.

My eyes open wide and I down mine too.

"I think I want another Screaming Orgasm, please," I say, not taking my eyes off his.

"Whatever the lady wants, the lady gets." He smiles.

While he's making the next couple of shots, I feel the warmth of it sliding down my throat. I also feel a warmth between my thighs that's spreading up inside me. I want him to give me a screaming orgasm for real.

He comes over and hands me my next shot and I see another couple lined up, ready to go.

I dare to be bold and lean over the bar. He leans towards me.

"Put your shot in your mouth and feed me your Screaming Orgasm, Hunter. Please." I kiss him on the cheek and then sit back down on my stool.

"Fuck, that's hot." I can see his desire for me in his eyes. He takes the shot and pours it into his mouth, then he leans over the bar towards me, pulling me towards him and he kisses me, all the while pouring his drink into my mouth.

When it's all in my mouth, he lets me swallow it then he devours my mouth. He presses his tongue in and it's like he's licking my mouth for the taste of the shot.

I pull away first because I feel like I'm about to spontaneously combust.

"Wow. That was fucking amazing," I say, sitting down and staring at him.

"You are so fucking hot. I can't move here. You'll have to talk to me about the weather or something." He points down to his groin

I sit up and look at his crotch. Smiling, I say, "Is that all for me?"

His face darkens. "This is all for you and no one else. This is what you do to me."

I smile.

"Hey, Hunter! Any chance of you doing any work tonight?" Keaton shouts from the other end of the bar, breaking our moment.

"Sorry, babe. I've got to go. Don't you move your pretty little arse from that chair. I'm going to spoil you tonight."

He walks down the bar to serve the queue of people.

While I sit there, I can hear the girls all saying they want a piece of Hunter. I smile to myself because I'm going to have him. Even if it is just once, I'm going to have myself my very own special piece of Hunter James.

HUNTER

I can't stop looking to the end of the bar. She is the most gorgeous girl in here tonight and she is *mine*. I know in my soul she's mine and she's always going to be mine. I just need to get past my issues with Grace. How do I know Scarlett is going to be different? That she isn't going to cheat on me with my best friend or anyone else? I don't. That's the hardest thing for me to accept.

I'm going to take each day as it comes, but I'm not going to rush into this relationship. I don't do relationships for a reason, but she makes me want to.

"Hey, Hunter," I hear someone shout. Turning to check out who said it, I see one of the girls from the other night watching me. She licks her lips.

When my eyes catch hers, she shouts, "What's the Hunter special tonight? Can I be the lucky woman?"

I look down to the end of the bar and Scarlett smiles at me. She doesn't look jealous or like she's going to fly off the handle. She just smiles and it's the most beautiful thing I've ever seen.

I shake my head. "Tonight is a special night. Tonight you'll be getting a Keaton special. I'm out of commission."

I hear some of the girls moan, but I don't care. I grab Keaton. "Hey, the girls want you, Keaton. Are you going to give them all Screaming Orgasms?"

He laughs. "I sure am." He scans the crowd and picks one of the ladies. "Come here, pretty lady. Do you want a Keaton special tonight?"

The pretty girl saunters up the bar, moving everyone else out of the way on her journey. I'm sure some of the other girls would stab her if they could get away with it.

She is just Keaton's type. Long brown, wavy hair, slim and gorgeous. I laugh to myself. Keaton doesn't realise his 'type' is the spitting image of his arch nemesis, Dakota. One day he might realise it, but tonight he can only see the beautiful woman in front of him.

He stands on the bar and helps the girl up, then he says, "Lay down on the bar." So she does.

He takes a shot glass and places it between her legs.

"This is going to be a bit different tonight. I'm going to drink the shot – from between your legs."

She gasps.

I make my way down the end of the bar where Scarlett is sitting, open-eyed, watching Keaton.

"Do you wish that was you up there?" I say, feeling something strange in my stomach.

She looks at me. "No way. I'd rather have one of your Screaming Orgasms any day."

My heart expands and I lean across the bar and kiss her. I could kiss her all night.

When we part, she goes back to watching Keaton on the bar. He's laid down too and is between the girl's legs, nudging her pussy with his nose as he attempts to drink the shot. It is pretty hot, to be honest.

When he's finished, everyone starts clapping and then they push their way to the bar. Keaton swaps numbers with the girl and tells her to stay and join him on his break. He's smooth. I taught him well.

Turning to Scarlett, I say, "I'm on break in a

few minutes. Do you want to get out of here for some fresh air?"

She looks at me like she's scared or something.

"What's wrong?" I reach over and touch her cheek. She leans into my hand. I fucking love it.

"I'm not going into your office where you fucked that girl last night, Hunter."

"Oh my God, I didn't mean that. I was going to take a walk along the seafront to get some fresh air. Scarlett, I know you're not that type of girl. You're different. You're special."

As soon as I've said that it's like watching a tightly wound coil, slowly unwind. She visibly relaxes and smiles at me. "Then I'd love to join you for a stroll," she says, in a really posh voice.

We both start laughing.

Keaton comes up behind me. "Will you take your break so I can get on mine quicker? This girl is hot to trot."

"You can go first, then I don't need to rush back after my break," I say, slapping him on his back.

He smiles. "Sure?"

"Yeah, I'm sure."

He leaves, dragging the girl from on the bar with him.

Scarlett looks a bit sad.

"What's the matter, Scarlett? I swapped because I don't want to rush our time together."

"It's not that. It's seeing Keaton going off with that girl. It reminds me of you and last night. I'll be fine. Just go serve those poor, thirsty girls and then you can walk me down by the sea."

I kiss her on the cheek once again and then go and serve the thirsty, horny girls.

ϒ ϒ ϒ

"Come on gorgeous," I say to Scarlett when Keaton is back and there's a lull in the bar. "Let's go for a walk." I come out from behind the bar, take her hand, and guide her through the bar and out the front door.

I didn't really think this through. As soon as I step through the front door, Zac is on me.

"You coming out the front instead of the back, Hunter? That's not your normal style."

"Fuck off, Zac," I say, wishing I could throttle him. "This is Scarlett." I hope to stop him from saying anything else to piss me off.

"We already met, didn't we, pretty lady?"

"We sure did," Scarlett says.

I look at her. She doesn't seem fazed by meeting my family.

Ainsley butts in, "I met her too. You've got a beautiful woman there, Hunter. You'd better treat her right."

I turn to face Scarlett and kiss her on the cheek. "I sure do and I certainly will. Come on. Let's get out of here. These two are cramping my style."

We cross the road and walk along the seafront, holding hands.

Okay, so this is a new concept to me and I thought it would feel strange, but it feels right. We come to the deckchairs where I met her earlier in the week and she goes to sit down.

"No. Don't sit there. I don't want to think about that bastard and the way he was treating you that night."

She smiles at me and walks over to the railings by the sea. I stand behind her and wrap my arms around her with her back to my front.

I nuzzle her neck and breathe her in. She smells tropical, like coconuts, and there's something else. It reminds me of the suntan oils we used to use when we were kids to get a really good tan. I smile at the memories of me and my brothers and sister having fun on the beach. That was when we were young and carefree.

"What are you thinking about?" she asks.

"Just remembering playing down here with my family. They were good days."

"Yeah, we used to come down here as well. I don't go to the beach these days. It seems like too much hassle."

"I know what you mean."

We don't say anything, but she leans backwards into me. My cock hardens from her brief touch and her beautiful aroma. I move my hips away because I don't want her to think I'm going to jump her bones or anything. Although, that's what I really want to do.

"Hunter, tell me how you came to have Mixology at such a young age." She leans backwards. It's like she wants every part of her body touching mine.

"I left Uni with no degree. Something happened and I had to leave. I went to Australia to learn how to become a mixologist. The first course I did was in Brisbane, and I loved it. Then I moved to Sydney, and the cocktails there were different again. I learnt a lot in the few years I was over there and then I got a letter from a lawyer telling me that the guy who had taught me in Brisbane, Victor, had died and left me some money. I knew I had been the best student and he kind of looked after me as I was eighteen and on my own, but I was shocked."

"You must have made a really good impression, Hunter. That is a big deal." She turns her face towards me and kisses me on the cheek.

"I know. I thought it was a scam at first, but I had to fly to Brisbane and meet with the lawyer. Victor left me enough to buy Mixology outright, renovate it, and enough money for me to be comfortable for the rest of my life. I decided to come home and open Mixology with my family. It might be mine on paper, but it's ours, really. We all have our part to play in the running of the bar and no decisions are made unless we all agree."

"That's amazing. You're amazing." She turns in my arms, wraps her arms around my neck, and brings my head down to kiss me.

Her kisses are like small shots of electricity powering through my body. They make me want to consume her and never leave her. When we break apart, I feel cold. It's like I need her to keep me warm.

"Mmm. You're not bad yourself." I kiss her again.

This time when we part, I take her hand and we walk back to Mixology. I don't let go of her hand until she's sitting in the seat she left earlier.

The rest of the night flies by, as it's really busy, and it's another successful night. I keep looking at Scarlett, and when I get a chance, I go over and talk to her. When the bar is closed and we've tidied up, it's time to leave.

"Can I walk you home?" I ask her, nervous she's going to say no.

"Why thank you." She laughs, curtseying. "That would be great." She blushes and looks down at the floor.

I lift her chin and kiss her.

"Come on," I say as we break apart. "Everyone ready?" I shout to the rest of the family. They all shout that they're ready to leave too. When I've locked the doors, I put my arm around Scarlett's shoulders and we walk towards where she lives.

"So, Scarlett, what do you do?"

"I'm a legal secretary for Harte, Wilson & Cooke."

"Really? They're my lawyers."

"No way? It's a small world."

We walk in relative silence and then she takes my hand and pulls me into an exclusive block of apartments.

"You live here? These are really nice."

"Are you coming in?" she asks me, blushing.

I think about it for a minute and then I say, "No. Not tonight. You're different to all the other girls, Scarlett. You've got under my skin and I like it. I never thought I would, so I don't want to ruin it by not treating you right."

She looks down at the ground and doesn't say anything. Then she slowly moves her head to look in my direction. "Don't you like what you see?" She asks with what looks like tears in her eyes. Fuck! I don't want her to cry.

"Of course I do. We got off to a bad start and I want to do things right. If I take you upstairs and fuck you then that's me being a bastard."

I push her against the wall and devour her. My resolve is starting to slip, but I want to do this right, not fuck her and then leave. I need her for more than that.

She pushes herself against me, rubbing my hardened cock in the process. "Hunter, please?" she whispers.

I can't do it. I can't stay. I want her so much. I feel a connection and I want more of it. I want it all.

"Scarlett, I want you so bad. You can feel how bad I want you," I say, rubbing my cock against her stomach. "I want you as a person more though. I need to prove to myself that this is not just about sex. Does that make sense?"

"Yeah, I suppose. I know it already." She smiles as she pulls away from me and walks through the door. She turns at the last moment. "Night, Hunter. Hope you have some dirty dreams about me." She turns and closes the door behind her.

I laugh. She is a naughty little minx.

I'm still laughing as I leave her building and start walking towards the seafront to get home. I'm not even five minutes away when I can hear someone behind me.

"Hunter!"

I turn to see who it is. There are two guys with black balaclavas on, staring at me.

"What the fuck? Who are you?"

They don't answer me, they just move closer.

I'm rooted to the spot. Who the fuck wants to hurt me?

"Didn't you get our message the other night?"

"You vandalised my bar?"

"Yeah, and now we're going to vandalise you." I see the iron bar just a few seconds before it hits me in the stomach. I bend over, winded. The second guy smacks me over the back and I'm useless against the two of them and the bars. They keep hitting me until I'm on the ground then one of them stands over me and says, "Maybe you'll understand this time." Then he kicks me in the face.

Y Y Y

I don't know how long I'm laid there, but I can feel someone trying to lift me.

"Are you okay?" I hear someone saying. "Oh my God."

I can't speak; it hurts too much. "Taxi," I mutter.

"I'll get you an ambulance. You need to go to hospital." He sits me up and leaves me leaning against a wall.

I hear him telling the controller that I need an

ambulance and he waits with me until they get to me. "Name?" I ask him.

He ignores me. "Good luck, Hunter," he says as the paramedics put me into the back of the ambulance. He must recognise me from the bar or something.

SLOE COMFORTABLE SCREW

1 1/2 Oz Sloe Gin, Orange Juice

What the fuck is that noise? It's a lot of beeping. I try to sit up but it hurts like fuck. Someone is in the room; a woman. She comes over to the bed.

"Good morning, Mr James. How are you feeling?" she says as she starts looking at things behind my head.

"What's going on?"

"You were brought into hospital last night. You've been beaten very badly," she says sympathetically.

"I need to get out of here." I try to get out of the bed.

"We're hoping you can get out later, but we

need someone to stay with you when you've gone home."

"That's fine. I have a very over-protective mother." I chuckle then realise it hurts too much. "My brother. I need to ring my brother."

"Give me his number and I'll ring him for you. We didn't know who to ring and it was so early this morning."

I give her Keaton's number and I know it won't be long before my peace is shattered.

Y Y Y

It takes Keaton about three quarters of an hour to round everyone up and get into the hospital. They all walk in behind him. That's one thing about my family… we would do anything for each other.

Mum rushes over to me and takes a deep breath in. "Hunter, what happened?"

"I wish I knew, Mum. I walked Scarlett home and then two guys jumped me. They were the same guys who vandalised Mixology the other night."

"Mixology was vandalised? Why don't we know about this?" Mum asks, looking at Dad.

"There was no need to tell you. We thought it

was a random attack," Keaton says, trying not to worry Mum.

Mum turns her attention to the nurse. "When can he get out of here?"

"He's going for some more x-rays first. We can send him home today, but we need to ensure someone will be with him all the time. We need the beds and it looks like he has enough people to care for him."

"He can stay with me," Mum says. I groan. I haven't lived with my parents for a long, long time.

"Mum, can we stay at mine please?"

She smiles at me. "We can, but if things get too hard then I'm taking you home." She leans down to kiss me.

I'm wheeled away for more x-rays and the doctors say I've broken a few ribs, a broken nose, and bruising to my face. Thankfully, they didn't break my jaw.

The doctor discharges me with some heavy painkillers and a letter just in case my ribs don't start to improve.

When we get home, I lie on the couch as Mum makes everyone tea.

"So, do you know who it was?" Zac asks, looking like he could kill someone.

"They admitted to vandalising Mixology, but I couldn't see them and I didn't recognise their voices. Who would do this to me?"

"It could be someone whose girlfriend you slept with. You know you never ask for their relationship status before you fuck them," Ainsley says, trying not to laugh.

"Fuck off, Ains," I say, laughing.

"It's not a bad suggestion. Who have you been with this week?" Keaton asks.

I look at him as if to say *are you joking?* I don't remember their names, and barely what they look like. Except for Scarlett.

I can feel the colour drain from my face.

"What?" Zac asks.

"Where's my phone? I need to ring Scarlett."

"Why?"

"When I first met her earlier this week, I interrupted her boyfriend being physical with her. She didn't want to go with him and I interrupted them, asking if she was okay."

Ainsley laughs. "How chivalrous. How stupid."

"I know, but I heard her saying no and couldn't let him push himself on her. It wasn't until she looked at me that I realised how beautiful she was, but she was happy to go off with him."

"She must have dumped him when she got home and then come and found you the next day," Ainsley says.

"I suppose." I ring Scarlett's number, but she doesn't answer. "She's not answering. She might be in work. Shit, where does she work?" I think for a minute. I'm feeling sleepy from the medication and my brain won't work. "Lawyer," I say, slurring.

"We can't go to the lawyer until we know who it is, Hunter," Mum says.

"No... Scarlett. Lawyer... Harte, Wilson & Cooke."

They look at me in confusion.

"WORK!" I shout as I start to fall asleep.

I can hear Keaton understanding as I drift off.

It's about two hours later when I wake up and there's only Mum and Ainsley in the apartment with me.

"Hey, where is everyone? Did they go to Mixology?" I ask, trying to sit up.

Mum helps me. "Not quite."

I look between her and Ainsley. "What's going on? Ains, tell me."

Ainsley sits down next to me. She clears her throat. "Keaton realised what you were saying about Scarlett and rang Harte, Wilson & Cooke looking for her. She hadn't turned up for work which, apparently, is unlike her. They said she's really conscientious and such a good worker."

I try to stand up. I have to go and see her, make sure she's okay. She didn't have that much to drink.

"Sit down, Hunter!" Mum shouts at me as I'm half way suspended above the couch. I slowly lower myself down.

"Skylar managed to get into your phone and find her number and did something to find where her phone was so they could go and make sure she was okay."

"And?" She's taking too long over this story. I need to know and I need to know now.

"They rang just before you woke up. They found her in some bedsit on the other side of town and she was beaten pretty badly. Skylar took her to the hospital and we're waiting to hear from him."

"I need to ring her, Mum. I need to know she's okay." I look around for my phone, but it's not there.

"They have your phone so they could find her. Skylar will bring it back. They took her phone too to see who she had last spoken to, and before Skylar went in the ambulance, he managed to track the location of a guy she had texted earlier in the week."

"Who is it?" I ask tentatively.

"We don't know, but Keaton and Zac have gone to find him, to see if he is the guy that vandalised Mixology. They think it was him and his friend who attacked you and Scarlett." Mum sits down and takes my hand.

I just want to cry. "Mum, how could anyone hurt her? She so delicate, gorgeous, and such an amazing person. I can't believe someone would do that to her. The fuckers!" I want to do something. I *need* to do something. I can't sit here waiting for someone to come back or ring me.

"If it helps, when the boys found her, she was asking for you. She was barely conscious, but she was asking for you."

That breaks my heart even more that I'm not there for my girl. It doesn't feel strange to call her that. She is my girl, and she will always be my girl.

Ainsley's phone rings and it's Skylar. "Hey, Sky," she says.

I reach over and grab the phone from her. "Sky, it's me. How's Scarlett? Tell me she's going to be okay."

"Hey, you woke up, you lazy sod. She's here with me. She had a sleep too. She looks worse than she is, to be honest. She doesn't have any broken bones or anything. They did slip her something so she can't remember anything."

"Did they…? Did they rape her?" I ask, worried about the answer.

"They've carried out tests and they don't think so. Hopefully they realised they were in trouble and just wanted to frighten her. She's asking for you. Are up to talking to her?"

"She's been awake this whole time and I'm wasting time talking to you? Put her on!"

Skylar laughs. "Love you too, brother."

"Hunter?" Scarlett whispers.

"Scarlett, baby. Are you okay?"

"I am now I know you're okay. I was so worried. They told me they were going to kill you."

"It takes a lot more than that to get rid of me. How are you doing?"

"I'm okay. I slept most of the drugs out of my system, thank God. I want to see you," she says tearfully.

"Me too. I want you to come here as soon as you can get out. Please."

"I should go home."

"Scarlett, please. I need to see for myself that you're okay. Mum won't let me leave here. I'm in a lot of pain."

She chuckles. "Okay. I'll stop in on my way home."

"No, I don't think you understand. You're not staying on your own. You can stay here."

"But, Hunter, we've just start…"

"Scarlett! I need to make sure you're safe. Just until those two fuckers are caught."

She laughs. "I didn't realise you were so bossy."

"You like that, don't you?"

"I've got to go. There's a doctor here."

"Hunter," Skylar says. "I'll ring you back when she's seen the doctor." He hangs up.

I lay back down on the couch and sigh. I'm wrecked.

Mum gives me another couple of painkillers and I slowly drift off. Again.

🍸 🍸 🍸

"Hunter. Hunter."

When I open my eyes, I see Scarlett sitting next to me and touching my face. As soon as her hand touches my face, I feel okay. I feel like I can take on the world.

"Hey," I say, touching her cheek. She leans into my hand as I lean into hers. "You came." I smile.

"I wasn't really given a choice." She laughs. A couple of tears escape from her eyes and roll down her face.

"Baby, I'll look after you. I'm so happy you're okay." I've never felt so emotional about someone in my life. Everything I went through with Grace has nothing on the emotions that are flowing through my heart right now.

"Tonight I'll look after *you*, Hunter." She leans down and kisses me gently on the lips.

I hear someone clear their throat. When I open my eyes, Mum is looking at me, smiling.

"Mum, this is Scarlett, but I'm sure you guessed that."

"Yes, I did. Nice to meet you, Scarlett." She holds out her hand. "My name's Verity."

"Nice to meet you too. Sorry about all of this. My ex-boyfriend is a nut job." She looks at me. "Skylar told you who they think it is. Keaton and Zac shouldn't go after him. He's trouble, Hunter."

"They can handle themselves, and anyway, we can't let them get away with it, Scarlett. Look what they did to you. That is unacceptable."

"I know. But I don't want your brothers to get themselves into trouble just because of me."

"Listen. You mean so much to me already. That means my brothers will take care of you too. Your problems are my problems. My problems are my family's problems. That's how the James family rolls."

"It sure is." Mum walks over to stand near us. "If Hunter wants you in his life, then we all want you in our lives. We're a very tight family and we never deal with a problem on our own. That has happened twice with my kids and it's not happening again."

Mum looks at me sadly. I know she's thinking of my bust up with Grace and my sudden departure to Australia without telling the family. Things were awkward for a while, but it didn't last long.

The second time was with Zac when he was in London.

Mum pulls Scarlett into a hug and I think she's shocked. I chuckle a little, but not too much because it hurts.

"Right, I'm going to cook some food for you all. It's been a long day already." She walks into the kitchen and I hear her open the fridge door. "Hunter, what the hell? Where's your food?"

I laugh. "I eat at your house or out so I don't have much."

"I'm going to the shop to get some. Come on, Ainsley. Let's get some food."

They both leave, and to be honest, I'm glad.

Scarlett looks at me and makes her way over to the couch. God, she's beautiful, even with all her bruises.

When she gets to the couch, she hesitates for a second, then she seems to make her mind up. She straddles me so she's sitting on my legs, facing me.

She reaches out and takes my face between her delicate hands and looks into my eyes. It's like she's looking for my soul. It's there for her to take. It's a few seconds before she leans forward and kisses me.

This isn't a hurried kiss of two lovers desperate to

shed their clothes. This isn't a kiss of two new lovers meeting for the first time. This isn't even a kiss which preludes sex. This is a kiss that tells me how she feels about me and how I feel about her. This is a kiss of love. Gut-wrenching, soul-seeking, ever-lasting love.

When she pulls away, she rests her forehead against mine. She closes her eyes. When she opens them again, she looks into my eyes. "Hunter, I'm scared."

I wrap my arms around her, as tight as I can without hurting myself. "Baby, I'm here. He's not going to hurt you."

"I'm not scared of him. I'm scared about us."

"Us? Why would you be scared of us?" I ask hesitantly.

"I don't want to be just a one night stand for you. That's what scares me. If I sleep with you, then you'll ditch me like you ditch all the other women. I can't do that to myself." She tries to get off my lap. I hold her in place. I can't let her walk away now or she won't come back.

"Scarlett, you are more than a one night stand to me. You've climbed under my skin and made yourself comfortable." She smiles. "I couldn't walk away from you, even if I was fully recovered. I feel you here." I place her hand on my heart. Fuck. When did I get all soppy?

"Really?" She looks at her hand on my chest and then back up to my eyes.

"Yes, really." I lean forward and kiss her, my hand snaking around to the back of her neck. Pulling her close, I slip my tongue inside her hot mouth. It feels like heaven and it sets off all these feelings in my body that I can't explain.

Y Y Y

Mum and Ainsley find us like that on the couch kissing.

"We can't leave you alone for two minutes, Hunter," Mum says, scolding me. I don't care; it was well worth it.

"Very funny, Mum."

Mum makes dinner and I ring Keaton to see what's going on and to tell them what time to be back for.

"Hey, Hunter. How are you? How's Scarlett?"

"I'm okay. My ribs hurt the most but I'll live. Scarlett is here with me. She's okay. More bruised than anything else. She was lucky."

"I know."

"What's the update, Keaton?" I take Scarlett's hand and she sits next to me, leaning in so she can hear too.

"Well, we've been looking for this Finn guy, but it's not as easy as we thought. Do you know who he is?" Keaton asks, concerned.

"No. I just know he was trying to force Scarlett into doing something she didn't want to do the other night. What else do I need to know about him other than he's a prick?"

"Give me that phone." I hear Zac in the background. There's a bit of shuffling. "Drive us back to Hunter's," Zac says to Keaton and then says, "Hunter, this is fucked up."

"What do you mean, Zac? What's going on?"

"He's disappeared. His family will be hiding him, no doubt. They are the Bridges from Hele. They own that turf and have been in a turf war with the Strickers for years. Hunter, this is gang territory we're getting into."

"Fuck!" I look at Scarlett. "Did you know who you were getting together with when you went out with him?"

"No. I met him in a pub and we went on a couple of dates before that night you showed up. He was trying to force me to kiss him and have sex with him and I didn't want to. I could tell he was shifty and I didn't want anything to do with him. That's why I dumped him. He wasn't happy about it and told me to watch out for myself. He must have been watching me and that's why he targeted your bar and you. I'm so sorry to bring all of this to your doorstep."

"Scarlett, don't worry about it. Honestly, you're worth any trouble that's thrown at us. We can handle ourselves."

I turn my attention back to Zac.

"So, little bro, what are we going to do about it?"

"Well, as you know, I have some friends who can help me out here. You know it's not legal, but I don't think that matters in this instance."

"Are these your friends from London?" I ask, hesitantly and quietly as I don't want Mum to over-hear me. She would panic if she thought Zac was even in contact with *those* friends.

"Yes. They have my back and I have theirs. It doesn't matter that I haven't seen or heard from them in two years. They're the ones who will help us, and quickly. I'm going to ring them now while Keaton is driving us to yours. After we've had dinner, we need to get Ainsley to take Mum home and then we can make some plans. Will Scarlett be up to this? She might have to get involved as she knows him better than we do."

I look at her and she nods her head.

"Yeah. She's in. But if she gets hurt, Zac, it's on your head. I don't care if you're my brother or not."

"Hunter, I got this. This is my speciality. I wouldn't let a woman get hurt ever. You know that."

"Yeah. Sorry, bro."

He hangs up and I take a few deep breaths.

"I'm sorry, Hunter," Scarlett says, trying to get away from me.

"Don't you go anywhere, baby. You're staying here with me, and after dinner, after we've planned our next move, I'm kicking everyone out and you and I are going to bed."

"I don't think you're up…"

I laugh. "I didn't mean that, but if you're offering, I'm always up for it. I just want to hold you in my arms in my bed tonight. That would make me feel so much better."

She kisses me and then we sit back and close our eyes for a few moments. It has been a busy day.

We're woken with a start when Zac crashes through the door. Even before he speaks, I know he's angry. He's a very aggressive man and his body seems to pump up when the endorphins flow through him like they are right now. He's looking for a fight and Finn is the one who needs to look out.

"What the fuck, Zac? You woke us up."

"Still sleeping, are you? You pussy. You should be out looking for whoever did this to your woman."

"Now now, boys," Mum says, diffusing the situation. "Hunter can't go out today; I won't let him. And you, my boy, need to calm down before you go charging after anyone and end up in prison. Now sit. Dinner is ready."

'Sorry, Mum," Zac says, calming down instantly.

We all sit at the table and talk about Keaton's upcoming championship that we want to go and watch.

"At least I'm not going up against Dakota this time," Keaton says. "She won't be anywhere near the place and I'm going to smash it." He smiles.

"Are you talking about Dakota Ryan?" Scarlett

says. We all turn to look at her. "Yes. Why? Do you know her?" Keaton asks.

"Yeah. I went to school with her. She's lovely."

"Are you sure we're talking about the same Dakota Ryan? The one I know is such a bitch!"

"Keaton James, you can't use language like that about a girl. That's just not right," Mum says, banging her fork down on the table.

"But, Mum, she is. She taunts me all the time. You know she's the bane of my life. I hate her."

We all start laughing; he really sounds like a spoilt child who keeps losing and is annoyed at the person who keeps winning. Actually, it is just like that.

"I'm supposed to meet her this weekend. She's going to watch some competition." Scarlett starts giggling. "Is that the one you're talking about?" She looks at Keaton's stricken face. "She keeps talking about this guy that she hates. He's her nemesis. She must be talking about you. Oh my God!"

"Keaton, this is too funny," I say, joining Scarlett in laughing.

"Right, you just laugh away. It's not like I've been helping you today at all, Hunter."

"Oh, yeah. Scarlett, stop laughing at Keaton.

It's not nice!" I say, trying to scold her without laughing.

She smiles and I can see she's trying to hold her laugh in. "Sorry. She really is a bitch. Oh, Keaton. You're so funny." Scarlett has tears running down her face. This is just what we all need.

When dinner is finished, the girls clean up and the rest of us sit down in the lounge to work out what we're going to do next.

"Now that I know his name, I can do some searches and see what I can come up with," Skylar says, reaching for the laptop. When he opens it, he starts clicking away on the keys. We're so used to hearing the clicking that we just ignore it and concentrate on what else we're going to do.

"I have my friends coming down to help out. When they heard it was the Bridges, they wanted in. They should be here in an hour. When Mum goes, we can let them in and sort this out once and for all," Zac says. He stands up and starts pacing the room. He's like a caged tiger, walking round and round just waiting to jump on his prey.

"Great. We need to find him and his mate." I say, worried this is all out of our league.

Scarlett comes back into the lounge and looks at me to see if can she come in and sit with us. I nod and she sits next to me. Ainsley follows her in and sits next to her. Mum stands looking at us all.

"I love my family. You all come together and look after each other. Just be careful and don't do anything stupid. I'm going home. Dad was away today and he's due back soon. Hunter, Scarlett, look after each other and rest." She walks over and kisses each one of us, including Scarlett.

Ainsley walks her to the door and then comes back to sit down. It's only about ten minutes later when Zac gets a call.

"Yeah. Okay. Meet you there." He hangs up. I guess his friends like to talk as much as he does.

"I'm heading out, guys. I'll catch up with you later. We need to open Mixology anyway so these guys are going to help me with security tonight – just in case," he says then turns and leaves.

"Yeah, I guess I'd better go too," Keaton says. "Come on, Ainsley. Some of us have work to do tonight."

She looks at us and kisses me on the cheek. "See

you later, Hunter. You'll be well enough to work in a couple of days."

"I've never had a day off since I started. This feels weird."

She laughs. "Time to get some you time then." They leave.

Skylar is still sitting there, clicking on the keys. When he looks up, everyone else has gone. "Hmm, suppose I'd better be going," he says, laughing. "I have a music booth to run. I might be onto something, Hunter. I'll check in with you if there's any news." He closes his laptop and stands. "See you later, Scarlett."

She surprises me as she stands and hugs him. "Thanks for taking care of me, Skylar. I really appreciate it." He blushes like mad and I snigger to myself.

"Yeah, um... see you later." He rushes out of the apartment.

Y Y Y

It's quiet when everyone has left.

"I thought they'd never leave," I say.

"I know. So, what do we do now? You need to

rest," Scarlett says, standing up again. "What can I get you?"

I look at her and feel my chest getting tight. I'm so lucky to have her in my life. She makes me feel whole again.

"I just want you. Then I'll feel better."

She smiles and reaches down to help me off the couch. "Come on, soldier. Let's get you to bed and I can take care of you," she says, before she realises what she said and blushes. "That's..."

"I know what you meant, and I think I like your idea better." I chuckle.

I take her hand and guide her into my bedroom. I've never had a girl here before; it's strange. She looks around and then I lay on the bed and she lays with me. She turns on her side, looking at me while I lay on my back.

She touches my cheek and then moves her finger slowly down my body.

"Scarlett, we don't have to do anything. I told you, I just want to hold you."

"I know, Hunter, and I want you to do that too, but I just keep thinking about Mixology," she says, not stopping her finger in its slow descent down my body.

"Why... why are you thinking of Mixology?" I

stumble over my words as her finger reaches my belt.

"Well, I know you can't work tonight so you're going to miss out on the cocktail of the day. What is it tonight?" She's now straddling my lower legs, looking up at me.

"Tonight… tonight is a Sloe Comfortable Screw." My eyes light up when I say the words.

"Hmm." She sits up and I feel the loss of her fingers.

She pulls her t-shirt over her head, wincing slightly as she does it. She pulls her hair to one side and knots it to keep it back. "I was thinking…" she says.

"What? What were you thinking?" I can't take my eyes off her tits. They're encased in a pretty, white, lace bra and spilling over the top. All I want to do is reach out and touch them. But this is her gig, and it would fucking hurt.

"I missed out on Monday night at Mixology, so how about we run through these cocktails. Monday was…"

I stare into her eyes. "The Blow Job," I say, gulping loudly as I think about her hot mouth around my cock.

"And Tuesday?"

"Cocksucking Cowboy."

"Hmm, and Wednesday was Slippery Nipple," she says, licking her lips. I was hard already, but now it physically hurts. It feels like my cock is going to bust out of my jeans. I moan as she reaches down and undoes my belt slowly. Too slowly. She lifts my hips and starts to take down my jeans and boxers.

"What about Thursday night? Oh, yeah. A Screaming Orgasm. I like the sound of that one."

"Me too." I moan, unable to do anything except watch her.

"What are the cocktails for tomorrow night and Sunday night?" she asks, pausing and looking up at me.

"Sex on the Beach and Happy Ending," I say, breathlessly.

"Ohh, I've never had sex on a beach. I like the sound of that. But let's not get ahead of ourselves. We've got enough to keep us going tonight anyway." She gives me a wicked grin.

"What are you going to do to me, Scarlett? You know I can't move a lot."

"I know that, that's what I'm counting on. If this is going to be a regular thing between us..."

"It is," I say quickly.

"Then I know for a fact I'm not going to be able

to get you at my mercy very often. I get the impression you like to lead and I bet you're alpha in the bedroom."

I smile. She knows me already.

"So, I'm taking this opportunity to do what I want to you, and you can't say no." She smiles, climbs off the bed, and takes my jeans and boxers off. I'm naked, exposed, and so fucking turned on by this woman in front of me that it hurts.

She takes her jeans and knickers off so she's also exposed and slowly climbs back on the bed. She crawls up my legs until her face is right above my cock.

I take a breath.

She takes my cock in one of her delicate hands. The feeling takes my breath away. Just her holding my cock could make me come; I'm so emotionally charged and turned on.

"You like that?" she asks.

"Do you think you need to ask? Can't you feel him straining in your hand?"

She smiles and leans down and, as well as moving her hand up and down my shaft, she opens her mouth and takes the tip of my cock into her mouth.

"Oh my God." That is the sweetest, hottest

mouth I have ever had wrapped around my cock. "Scarlett."

She doesn't answer me, she just keeps taking my cock deeper and deeper. But she's doing it slowly, making me wait until I hit the back of her throat. Then she moans and it drives me insane. The vibrations of her moan send me into a frenzy. I want to thrust in her mouth and speed her up; she's being too slow. I need to come in her mouth. Oh God, how I want that.

She pulls her mouth off my cock and looks me in the eye. "You're big. I didn't think I would be able to take you so deep. I think I'm going to have to try again just to make sure it's not a fluke." She winks at me and then lowers her mouth again.

"Baby, that is no fluke. God, Scarlett, what are you doing to me?"

She starts to take her mouth off my cock again and then moves her hand up and down my shaft and takes me into her mouth at the same time. I don't know which sensation is driving me mad, or if it's both.

Her free hand starts to trace a finger under my balls and down towards my arse. That really sensitive spot at the bottom of my balls. Oh God. Then she takes her mouth off my cock again and slides down the bed a bit. She takes my balls into her mouth.

"Fuck, Scarlett." No one has done that to me before. Boy, have I been missing out. One hand is moving up and down my shaft, the other is tracing from my balls to my arse. I can't think straight with all these emotions. All these feelings. All these sensations.

"Scarlett, I'm going to come if you don't stop soon." I growl.

She lifts her head and smiles. Then she moves her body up a fraction and takes my cock into her mouth, using one hand on the shaft and the other to jiggle my balls. She is driving me insane.

"Scarlett, you need to stop. I'll come."

"That's what I want," she says, with my cock still in her mouth.

It's too much for me to bear. I warned her.

"Fuck!" I shout as I shoot my load down her throat. I can still feel her hand on my shaft, her finger under my balls and her beautiful, hot mouth around me. She takes me really deep as I come like I've never come before and I hear her gulping to take it all.

After a couple of seconds, when I stop shooting

it down her throat, she pulls her mouth off my cock and groans for air.

"Oh God. I was losing consciousness there. I couldn't breathe," she says, flopping down beside me.

"Baby, that was amazing. The best blow job ever."

"Good," she says, catching her breath. "I've not finished yet. I realise you need time to recuperate, so it's my time."

I don't understand because I can't really go down on her with my ribs hurting so much. She leans over me and kisses me deeply. I can taste myself on her and it feels dirty. She straddles my waist but doesn't sit down. Then she moves slowly up my body, removes my pillow from behind my head and straddles my face.

"I'm going to ride your face now. Do your worst," she says as she lowers herself so that her pussy is directly over my mouth. She holds onto the headboard. "I'm in charge here, Hunter. I determine the pace. If it gets too much for you then shout, okay?"

"Baby, I have a feeling I could eat your pussy all day, every day."

"Shut up, Hunter, and lick me."

She lowers herself fully onto my face. I raise my arms so that they're around her legs and I can pull her lips apart. I lean up and lick her. I moan. She tastes so good and she is so wet for me.

"God, that feels so good. Hunter, moan again," she says as she pushes her pussy even closer to me.

I do what she wants and lick her and then I plunge my tongue inside her. My nose is touching her clit and I'm rubbing it, then I moan, and moan, and moan.

"Fuck. Fuck. Fuck!" She comes all over my tongue. I didn't even put a finger inside her.

When she stops pushing her pussy closer to my face and calms down from her orgasm, she lifts herself off me and lowers her body down mine. She looks at me shyly.

"Sorry about that, but sucking your cock and then feeling your tongue inside just sent me over the edge. It's been a while." She blushes.

"How can you sit there and blush when you just did what you did." I laugh, take her face in my hands, and devour her mouth. I can taste her and I hope she can taste it.

She reaches behind her and feels my heavy, hard cock poking her. "I see you're ready to go again." She smiles as she lifts herself off me.

"Scarlett, you're going to kill me."

"No, Hunter. I just want to ride my cowboy." She turns herself around so that she's facing the bottom of the bed, still straddling me. She takes my cock in her hand and then positions herself over the top, but then she stops and turns to face me, smiling.

"Oops. Hunter, you're driving me insane. I nearly forgot. Where are your condoms? I need to have your cock inside me, so tell me quick."

"Top drawer, left side." She climbs off, reaches into the drawer and pulls a few out, and after taking one, she throws the rest on the bed, looking at me and smiling. "For later."

Who is this girl? She is going to fuck me to death.

She opens the packet and rolls the condom on my cock and then lowers herself down on top of it.

"Oh my God, Scarlett. You're going to kill me. You are so fucking tight."

She sits there and doesn't move for a minute.

"Are you okay, baby?" I ask her, worried. "You don't have to do this if you don't want to." I don't know how I would be able to pull out of the tightest, hottest pussy I have *ever* had, but if she wants me to then I can.

"Just give me a minute. You're huge, Hunter."

I laugh. I take the moment to touch her arse, which is clearly in my view and spread out over my cock. I push her cheeks together and then spread them out so I can feel the movement on my cock.

"Okay, are you ready?" she says, as if she was waiting for me.

"I'm not sure what for, but hell yeah!" I laugh.

She leans forward and starts lifting her arse quickly, and she fucks me with abandonment. I have never felt anything so good in my whole life.

"Hunter, fuck that feels good." She turns to face me.

"Scarlett, don't stop whatever the hell you're doing because, that is amazing."

She doesn't slow down. At all. All I can see is her arse bobbing up and down my cock and all I want to do is push her so that she's on all fours and I'm ramming my cock into her tight pussy, but I can't. This is her show. And my ribs are so sore.

"Baby, I'm going to fucking erupt in a minute," I say.

She stops, leans back, and I kiss her. Then she climbs off.

"What the fuck? Where are you going?" I ask her, confused.

She smiles and turns to face me. "I want a slow, comfortable screw, please. Will you give it to me?" She has one of her little fingers at the edge of her mouth like the minx she is.

I want nothing more than to make love to this girl. I can feel all my emotions coming to the surface and I want to show her how much I want her.

I reach out, grab her, and pull her down to me so that she's laid on top of me. "Fuck that hurts." I say, pissed off.

"Do you think you can go on top? Then you can set the pace and if it hurts too much we can do something else. I need your cock and I want your orgasm so much." When I look at her face, I realise I would do anything for her.

"Move over," I say, pushing her off and getting her underneath me.

She spreads her legs for me and it is singlehand-edly the most beautiful sight I have ever seen. I lean over her. It hurts, but I really don't care. I want to be back inside her and I want to make love to her. She's fucked me already and I want to show her how much I care.

I push my cock inside her sweet pussy and she clenches me again. It feels tight, like I've never been inside, and I watch as her eyes roll to the back of her head. "Fuck, Scarlett. This feels like coming home."

I slowly fuck her, taking my time to pay attention to her lips, her tits, and her nipples with my mouth. I'm kissing her when I need to speed up; I can feel the tension coming from the soles of my feet and spreading up my body to my balls.

"Baby, I'm going to come. I can't hold on anymore."

"Hunter," she says. "Fuck me!"

That's all I can take. I lean back and pull her legs up around my shoulder. Fuck the pain. I ram inside and fuck her until she comes around my cock and I explode inside her.

It takes me a couple of minutes to finish coming and all I can see is stars in front of my eyes. When I know she's finished too, I take my cock out and roll off her. I don't even have the energy to take the condom off. I lay down beside her.

"My God, that was the most amazing experience of my life. I'm not letting you go, you know that, don't you?" I say, pulling her into my body.

"I don't want you to let me go, Hunter. I want to stay here with you."

6

SEX ON THE BEACH

1 1/2oz Vodka, ¾ Peach Schnapps, 1/2oz Crème De Cassis, 2oz Orange Juice, 2oz Cranberry Juice

We got up last night, cleaned ourselves off, and Scarlett gave me my painkillers then we climbed into bed and I had the best night's sleep ever. It feels like Scarlett is a dream; she can't be real. When I try to roll to my side, the first thing I do is wince. The second is smile when I see her beside me with her hair fanned out, and she's smiling in her sleep.

I can't help myself. I trace my finger down her cheek to her lips and then I gently turn her head to face me. I lean over and gently kiss her on the lips. She opens her eyes and smiles. "Hey," she says.

"Hey, gorgeous. Did you sleep well?"

"I should be asking you that."

"I had the best night's sleep ever. It's only because you were in my bed. I think you'll have to stay every night from now on," I say, trying to keep a straight face.

"Oh, you do, do you?" She laughs and turns on her side. She runs her hand down my chest. "What if I didn't sleep well? Then I could never sleep here again."

I grab her hand. "That is not happening, Scarlett."

She laughs again and I feel her relax into me. "What's going on between us, Hunter?" she asks nervously.

"I don't know. You've come into my life and turned it upside down in a matter of days. But I know that I don't want this to end. I want you. I need you. I haven't needed anyone who isn't family for so long. I never wanted anyone to come into my life and make me rely on them. I don't want to risk my love again."

"What happened before? I know something did. You're with a different girl every night and then these last few nights you've been spending time with me and you seem so different to the image you portray. You like to be a playboy, someone who fucks anything in a skirt. But I sense that you just want someone to love you."

I put my arm above my head and rub my eyes. "I went through a really bad break up in Uni and I don't trust people."

"What happened?"

"Urgh, I hate talking about it, but it was the reason I went to Australia before I finished and the reason I don't do relationships. Until now." I say smiling at her. I met this girl, Grace, and I thought she was everything I wanted in a girl. We were the talk of campus and everyone wanted to be our friend. We were together nearly a year and a half when we had a party at our house and everyone got totally wasted. I couldn't find her so I went looking for her and when I went into our bedroom, she was lying naked on the bed." I take a deep breath. Thinking about this just makes it all come back to me.

Scarlett squeezes my hand. "Hunter, you don't have to tell me. It's not really my business."

"I do need to tell you. I don't want any secrets with you and I want our relationship to work, so you need to know." I take another deep breath. "At the side of the bed, being pulled down on top of her, was my best friend, Cooper. He was about to fuck her. In my bed. My girlfriend." I can feel myself getting angry.

Scarlett kisses me on the edge of my lip. "What did you do?"

"I shouted at the two of them and told them to fucking have each other then I grabbed a bag and threw some things in and left. I went straight to the airport and took the next plane out of there, which just happened to be to Australia. The rest is history."

"Did you hear from either of them again?"

"Cooper was messaging me, telling me that I had it wrong, that he wasn't going to fuck her. He said that she was trying to seduce him and he was telling her no. Not that it looked like that to me. Grace messaged me telling me that Cooper was coming on to her and it was all his fault. They were than welcome to each other. Thankfully, moving to Brisbane was the best thing that ever happened to me. Except meeting you, of course."

"Hunter, that's terrible, being betrayed by the two closest people to you. I won't betray you. I promise."

I kiss her. "I know. Being with you feels so different than being with Grace. I know now that deep down I didn't really love her. But it fucking hurt to be betrayed by the two people I cared for the most."

We're silent for a short while then Scarlett says, "Thanks for telling me, Hunter."

"I won't hide anything from you. But I might get jealous, just so you know."

"Don't worry. If you're jealous then it means you like me a lot." She smiles and then kisses me. "Come on, lazy bones. We need to get up and find out what Finn is up to."

All I want to do is drag her back into the bed with me for some more of what she did last night. She fucking rocked my world.

Y Y Y

After breakfast, Zac and his friends let themselves into the apartment. Keaton isn't coming as he has to do some last minute training for his championship tomorrow. Skylar comes in and sets up his laptop.

"Hey," Scarlett says to them. We must look a right pair with all our bruises.

Scarlett makes coffee for everyone and then we sit around the dining table. "What's going on, Zac?"

I ask tentatively, as I'm not sure I really want to know what they were up to last night.

"We went to the Underground last night."

"What's that?" Scarlett asks.

"It's a fight club." I say. "Not somewhere you want to be going."

She just nods her head.

"Zac, you know you shouldn't be going there."

"I know, but I needed to do this for you, bro. Don't worry; I won't be going back in a hurry. We're going to close this down today."

We spend the next hour talking about Finn and his family. Zac says that we need to do this legally so there is no retaliation. I thought he might have gone in half-cocked, looking for a fight, but it seems he really has changed.

Skylar does some searching on his laptop and finds where Finn is. Scarlett says she knows the place and tells us what she knows about Finn.

We agree Scarlett is going to go in there and accuse him of beating me up. I don't like the idea, but she says she wants to do this for me. She's going to record the conversation so that when he agrees with her, then we can swoop in and take Finn down.

They don't want me to go with them because of my injuries and it would look more realistic if she goes on her own. I don't know if I can sit here and wait for her to come back so I agree to go with Skylar to meet Ainsley at Mixology and do some planning for tonight. I'm not going to work tonight, but there's always shit that needs to be done, and it will be better to keep my mind occupied when Scarlett has gone.

Everyone leaves to wait outside while I say goodbye to Scarlett.

"Baby, you don't need to do this, you know? The boys can get him."

"Hunter, I want to do this for you and for all the other women he thinks he can just hit around when it doesn't go his way. He can't get away with that."

"I know, but I don't want you getting hurt anymore."

"He can't hurt me. Zac and the boys will be on the other side of the door. They will come and get me before anything bad happens. I promise. Tonight I'll be staying with you all night. After all, tonight is Sex on the Beach night and you know I haven't done that!" She kisses me.

I've never been so worried before. But I have to trust her. She wants to do this.

"Baby, I'll be waiting at Mixology. You ring me as soon as it's over and get your arse back to me.

I'm not losing you now. I've just got you," I say, grabbing her and kissing her as if my life depends on it.

"I'll be fine. Stop worrying. Just think about tonight and me staying over again." She winks at me as she walks through the door to go and meet the guys.

Skylar brings me to Mixology and he starts getting organised for tonight. As it's Sex on the Beach night, he's going for a Hawaiian Hula theme with the music. Ainsley and I look over the figures for the week so far and we see it has been a resounding success.

"Hunter, you know, we're going to have to do this a couple of times a year. These figures are through the roof. Let's hope these customers keep coming back regularly and don't just dwindle away."

"I know. It's been amazing and so much fun."

"Well, you definitely had fun at the beginning of the week. The end of the week hasn't been as much fun for you," she says, wrapping her arms around me and hugging me.

"Ainsley, the end of the week has been the best two days of my life. Apart from being beaten up, of course."

"So, you really like Scarlett then? I don't think I've seen you so happy in so long. If she's putting that smile on your face and continues to do so, then I'm really happy for you. I know why you don't like to do relationships and it sucks. Being betrayed is not a nice experience for anyone, but do you know what? You made the best decision by leaving for Australia. We were all so sad to see you go, but it was fate, Hunter."

"Yeah, I believe that now too. Our paths are already written and something has to happen to make you choose the right path. I was meant to stumble upon Scarlett and Finn the other night. Little did I know how important she would be in my life."

"You've fallen for her bad, haven't you?" Ainsley touches my arm.

"Yeah, I have. If anything happens to her today, I don't know how I could live with myself."

"She'll be fine. Look, after what happened to Zac in London, there is no chance she will get hurt. You know how overprotective he is and she's a woman. Believe me, she's in the best hands possible with him."

"I know. I'm just worried. I can't lose her now."

"God, Hunter, you are seriously being soppy. I hope it's the drugs and not you losing your man card." She laughs and walks away.

We go back into the bar and start setting things up. It hurts to carry some of the stuff around, but I can cope. It helps to take my mind off Scarlett and Finn.

SCARLETT

I know Hunter said I don't have to do this, but really I do. I can't live with myself if Finn keeps hurting Hunter and I. I winked at Hunter when I left, but it was the last thing I wanted to do. I am so nervous. I get into the back of the Zac's car and have to squeeze in next to Zac's friend and then the other one climbs in beside me. I don't know their names and I'm not sure I want to. They are as scary as hell, big muscles, big necks and all they do is grunt.

Zac is the first one to speak. "Scarlett, is there

anything you want to tell us about Finn? Anything we need to know about him?"

"I … I don't know much about him. I hadn't been with him long."

He doesn't say anything else.

We drive to the location Skylar gave us and Zac parks away down the road a bit. He turns the engine off and then turns in his seat to look at me.

"You can still walk away Scarlett. We can just go in there and rough him up a bit, he'll get the message."

I gulp. I can only imagine what they would like to do to him.

"I have to do this. He needs to hear it from me."

"Okay, if you're sure. This is what is going to happen …"

Zac tells me that I need to go into the garage first and accuse Finn of beating me and Hunter. I am shaking so bad I think I am going to be sick. Zac leans over the seat and takes my hand. "We will be just on the other side of the door. We will hear what is going on and you just need to say my name and I will come in and take over the situation. Gavin here will bring you out and make sure you are safe in the car. Understand?"

I nod my head. "Yeah."

Gavin gets out of the car to let me out and the guys follow. I walk ahead of them and just as I am about to open the door Zac grabs my arm. "I've changed my mind, I don't want you to go in there."

"Why not?"

"He's too dangerous. I don't know what I was thinking about sending you in there."

"He won't hurt me."

"He beat you up before. He will do it again."

"Zac, I want to do this. I know you have my back and I know that you won't let him hurt me."

He's quiet for a minute then he nods his head. "Okay, but any sign of trouble and we are right behind you."

"I know you are." I lean up and kiss his cheek. "Thanks Zac."

Turning away from him, I open the door to the garage and walk in. "Finn!" I shout.

It doesn't take him long to come out of the office. "What are you doing here?" He shouts as he comes over to stand next to me.

"You're a bastard. Beating me up and then doing the same to Hunter. You make me sick."

"You love it." He says, trying to touch my arm. I step back out of his reach.

"No, I don't."

"Well he's nowhere to be seen so we got him really good. Didn't we?" He says, puffing his chest out and looking proud.

"He is fine. Stay away from both of us."

"Both of you? You're an item are you? I thought you would come running back to me when you saw what a pussy he was. He laid on the floor and accepted the beating we gave him."

"You had steel bars for fucks sake." I scream at him.

He steps closer.

"Yes, we did and it was fun to watch him squirm. Now you on the other hand. We could have had so much fun with you that night, but you weren't the main prize. He was."

"You make me sick."

He laughs, like a maniac. "I know you want me." He says taking my arm and pulling me towards him. My back crashes into his chest and he says in my ear, "Can you feel how hard you make me? You need to sort that out now." He starts thrusting his hips into my arse and I can feel his cock rubbing against me.

"Get. Off. Me." I shout, with gritted teeth.

He grabs hold of my hair and tilts my head by

pulling on it. He tries to grid his mouth down on mine but I bite his lip.

"Bitch!" He shouts as he slaps me.

"What's going on?" I hear someone else say. "Ooh look who came out to play." He says walking towards us.

Now I'm scared. He circles us and sees blood on Finn's lip. He nods his head towards me. "She do that?" He asks Finn.

"She sure fucking did."

"I told you we should have fucked her the other night." He stands in front of me and says, "Worst mistake you made coming here sweetheart."

Staring into his eyes I can easily believe it if it wasn't for the four guys on the other side of that door.

"ZAC," I scream.

"What the fuck?" Finn shouts before loosening his grip on me.

As the door bursts open and the four biggest men I have ever seen in my life come in, Zac zero's in on me. "You okay?"

"Yeah."

"Go get in the car and wait for us." He looks at the Finn and his friend. "We won't be long."

I run as fast as I can out of the garage and jump

into the back seat of the car. My heart is racing and I am really scared.

As the reality of what Finn and his friend were saying sinks in I can feel the tears starting to well up. They were going to rape me the other night. They wanted to do that now. If Zac wasn't there they would have raped me.

I cry until I have no more tears and then the four of them come out and climb into the car.

No-one says a word. Zac just drives us to the police station and I press charges. Zac is there with me and is beside me at all times. He is like my personal bodyguard. He doesn't say much, but his actions speak louder than words. I don't think I can thank him enough.

HUNTER

It feels like hours before they come back and Scarlett runs into my arms and starts crying.

"Hey, baby. I'm so happy you're back. Are you okay? It's okay."

"Hunter it was awful," she says between sobs. "He was so aggressive from the moment I got through the door. He didn't suspect though, and he admitted it all to me. He was even gloating about it because he said he hadn't seen you around so thought he had done a good job on you."

"Shh, it's okay. He didn't hurt you, did he?" I ask, getting angry thinking about him putting his hands on her.

"No. He was going to, but Zac stormed through the door and stopped him."

I look around and see Zac and give him a nod of my head. He nods back. He'll tell me everything later. She pulls back from my hug.

"It looks great in here. Are you working tonight?"

"No. I'm going to take the night off and then work tomorrow night. Is that okay with you?"

"Of course it is. I thought you might want to stay here tonight and work. But I'm so happy you don't want to. I get you to myself again." She smiles at me with innocence, but I know different.

I laugh at her and pull her into another hug. This time I kiss her. I'm so happy she's okay. "I need to talk to Zac and then we can get out of here," I say, and she wanders off to find Ainsley.

"Hey, Zac. What's the story? Do you want to tell me what happened?" I sit down with him and his mates.

"It went exactly to plan. Your girl is amazing. She wasn't nervous at all. She just marched straight in there and accused him of beating you up, and the stupid fucker was proud of it. He thought she would like it and want to be with him again. When he realised she didn't, he started getting aggressive and shouting at her. But she stood her ground and got him to admit it all. Then she shouted my name and we ran in there and got her out. We got him and his mate on the ground and we might have accidentally kicked him a few times before we rang the police. That's where we've been. Scarlett pressed charges and we told them that you would too, so they want to see you later on."

"Thanks, bro. Thanks for looking after her for me."

"That's what us James' do. You looked after me when I needed it." He hugs me. It's so uncharacteristic that I'm taken aback, but then I take his hug.

I look over at his mates. "Thanks, guys. Really appreciate it. Are you staying for a while? Drinks are on the house."

"Thanks, Hunter. We'd like that. It's been a while since we saw Zac and we'd love to catch up," Trey says.

"I'm working tonight, but as Hunter says, drinks are on us," Zac says.

Y Y Y

A few hours later, after spending time in the police station giving a statement, and having dinner, I'm on my balcony, looking out to the sea with Scarlett in my arms in front of me. "Hunter, this really is beautiful. It's so peaceful. I could stand here for hours."

"I know. Me too."

"You know, tonight is Sex on the Beach night." She pushes her arse into my crotch.

"I know, baby. I'm too relaxed to go all the way down to the beach. We've had a busy day."

She leans back on me and I wrap my arms tighter around her. "You know, I could get used to this."

"What do you mean?"

"Standing here with you. Looking at this amazing view."

"You want me for my view, do you?" I say, laughing.

"Who said I want you?" She rubs her arse all over my hard cock.

I run my hand down her flat stomach and into her jeans. Then I push it further down into her knickers. She's wet. "This tells me you want me. You're wet for me. All for me." She moans and it's one of the best sounds in the world. I plunge a finger inside her wet, hot, pussy. She moans some more. I lean forward to whisper in her ear. "You want me. You can't deny it. Your pussy was meant for me, Scarlett." I bite her earlobe.

She moans and says, "I want you, Hunter. Right here. Right now." She undoes her jeans and pulls them down, along with her knickers. Fuck, she is so sexy.

"Right here? Right now?" I ask as I pull my jeans and boxers down.

"Yeah. Let's have a 'Sex on the balcony looking at the beach' kind of a night." She laughs.

I push her forward slightly, grab her hips, and pull them back so she opens up for me. I run my finger down between her lips. "You're so wet for me, Scarlett. I can't wait to taste you again. But right now, I just want to sink my rock hard cock into your hot, tight pussy."

"Do it, Hunter. Don't just talk about it. Do it."

I don't give her a chance to say anything else. I spread her cheeks apart so I can see where my cock has to go and I slam straight into her. "Fuck, you're tight," I say. I wait for a minute to adjust to her tightness around my cock.

"Hunter." She pushes her arse back further onto my cock.

That's enough to send me into a tailspin. I pull out almost all the way and then slam straight back inside. She moans. Fuck, I love that sound already.

"Don't let anyone know what we're up to. The lady downstairs is coming out onto her balcony. Don't make a noise, Scarlett." She nods her head in agreement and then it's game on.

I fuck her relentlessly. She feels so good around my cock. This is where she belongs. This is where I belong. "Hunter," she whispers. "I'm going to come." That small piece of information doesn't make me slow down; in fact, I speed up.

She screams my name as she comes all around my cock. She has it squeezed tight so it feels like it's in a vice. I explode inside her and it feels like heaven. As I start to calm down, I say, "I thought you were supposed to stay quiet."

"I know." She laughs. "But I couldn't help myself."

I'm leaning against her back, trying to catch my breath. When I slide out of her, I realise that I didn't use a condom. "Fuck! Sorry, Scarlett. I got carried away. I didn't use a condom."

I feel her go tense as she tries to digest this piece of information. "I'm on the pill and I'm clean. What about you? I know you're erm … very active!"

I hate that she knows I'm a player and that I've fucked most of the women in this town. It makes me feel cheap and dirty. After having fucked her, I wish I could wipe those women from my past, but I know I can't. "I *was* but I always use protection. You caught me unaware and for the first time in my life I didn't think about anything except getting inside you. I'm clean Scarlett, I have regular tests."

She turns in my arms, and pulls up her jeans and mine. She wraps her arms around my neck and pulls me down. "Shut up and kiss me, Hunter," she says and kisses me like her life depends on it.

7

HAPPY ENDING

2oz Mandarin Vodka, 4oz Club Soda, 2 Splashes Cranberry Juice

Once again, I wake up with Scarlett in my arms. I slept well again last night and I'm feeling much better. I want her to stay here forever. That should frighten me, but surprisingly, it doesn't. I pull her to me and kiss her cheek. She starts moving backwards to get as close as she can.

"Morning," she says, sticking her arse out and rubbing my cock.

I laugh. "Not this morning, gorgeous. We have to go and support Keaton today."

"Oh, yeah. I'm meeting Dakota down there."

I laugh. "Keaton is not going to be happy with

her being there and you knowing her just makes it hilarious." I climb out of bed and walk to the kitchen to put on coffee. Scarlett follows me.

"What's the deal between the two of them, Hunter?"

"Keaton is really good at surfing and has won loads of local competitions and wants to go pro. The only thing stopping him is Dakota Ryan. They seem to take it in turns to beat each other, each of them spurred on by seeing the other lose." I hand her a cup of coffee and we walk out to the balcony. I can't help but think of last night out here and I smile to myself.

"Dakota won the Cornish Championships two weeks ago and that means that she's representing Cornwall in the UK Championships in a few weeks. This is Keaton's chance to win the Devon Championships and compete against her in the UK Championships." I take a sip of my coffee and linger over the smell that wafts up my nostrils.

"So, who is better? Dakota or Keaton?" Scarlett asks with a wicked smile.

"I have to say Keaton because he's my brother, but Dakota really is amazing. They've had lots of practice this year and it will be touch and go who wins."

"Well, this could get awkward, because I might have to cheer for Dakota, you know? Will Keaton hate me?" She looks at me with puppy dog eyes.

I lean forward and kiss her on the lips. "How could anyone hate you? But he might be pissed off." I laugh. "Come on. We have to get ready and be down in Bantham in an hour. We're meeting the rest of the family down there. Are you okay to go on the back of my bike? The journey is beautiful and best seen on a Ducati Diavel. Are you game?"

"I've never been on a bike before, but as long as it's with you, then I'm game."

"Great," I say, standing up and kissing the top of her head. "Let's get dressed. We have to go."

I've ridden my bike hundreds of times, but this is the first time I've had someone on the back. It was always a time for me to regroup and think about everything. A time when I could get lost in the wind blowing in my face and the sea air deep in my lungs. I love the feeling of the wind against me as I ride down the coast, but having those two gorgeous arms wrapped around my waist and holding on for her life makes me feel the happiest I have in years.

When we arrive in Bantham, we park up, and Mum, Dad, Ainsley, and Zac are waiting for us. Skylar had to go to an exhibition in Birmingham so he can't make it today. He'll be at the championships though, that's for sure. None of us would miss that for the world.

Everyone has already met Scarlett, except for Dad, and I introduce her to him. "This is my dad, Jack."

"Good to meet you, Scarlett. I hope you're feeling better. You're in safe hands with Hunter."

"Thank you. I am feeling better and your whole family has been amazing."

"Come on. Let's go and find our places for watching Keaton beat them all," Dad says.

"Erm… I need to go and meet my friend," Scarlett says, obviously embarrassed.

I start laughing. "You are never going to guess who her friend is," I say to Dad.

He shakes his head.

"Dakota fucking Ryan, as Keaton calls her." I can't stop laughing; this is just too funny. I pull her into a hug. "It's fine, Scarlett. Go meet her and we will catch up later."

Y Y Y

It's about an hour before the competition starts and it looks like Keaton is in the middle of all the surfers. Scarlett walks over to where we're sitting with the stunning Dakota. She isn't my type, of course, but I can see her appeal.

"Is it okay if we sit with you?" Scarlett asks.

"Of course it is. Hey, Dakota," I say, indicating for them to sit down.

They sit in front of us and I keep touching Scarlett's shoulder, just so she knows I'm still here. Keaton is due up next and we're all getting excited.

He looks fantastic paddling out to catch the right wave. I am so proud of him and he knows that if he doesn't win today, we will always back him.

As he jumps on his board, we all stand to watch his every move. I don't understand all the different terminology or sayings that the surfers seem to use, but what I do know is that Keaton is kicking the waves' arse. He looks amazing and he's staying on his board much longer than the others who have surfed before him.

Dakota is jumping up and down and shouting his name as much as Scarlett is. He gets perfect scores, but it isn't until after the last one has surfed that we get really excited. Even though surfing is all about skill, it's also about catching the perfect waves, and sometimes Mother Nature doesn't want to play ball.

They are announcing the winners and we're all so excited when we hear Keaton's name being called for winning overall.

"Go on, Keaton!" I scream, I can't wait to hug him. He's my brother and I'm so proud of him right now. Even Scarlett and Dakota are jumping up and down with joy.

When Keaton has finished talking to everyone, he wanders over to us, but his face falters when he realises Dakota is with us.

"What the fuck are you doing here? Isn't it bad enough that you have to breathe the same air as me, let alone stand with my family? What the fuck, Dakota?"

"Keaton!" Mum shouts at him, but Keaton can't see anyone else around him except Dakota.

She is getting mad as she moves closer to him. She is shaking her head and I think I see tears in her eyes. All of a sudden Scarlett stands between the two of them with Dakota at her back and pushes Keaton. "Keaton James, I may have only known you a few days, but this is not the Keaton I know. What the fuck is your problem? Dakota is my friend. I am dating your brother." I smile when she says that. Yes, she sure is dating me. "I'm going to be around you and family for a long time, so you need to get used to being in the company of my friends as well. You did a lot for me this week and I'm eternally grateful. Why don't you try showing Dakota that side of you and she might stop thinking you're an arsehole. Mind you, right now, you are being an arsehole!"

Keaton stumbles backwards. I start clapping, and if I didn't know it already, then that moment sealed the deal for me. I'm falling in love with Scarlett faster than the speed of sound.

Keaton looks at me, and then Zac, Ainsley, and my parents start clapping. "Well said, Scarlett. And well done, Keaton. Scarlett is right though. Dakota was cheering you on to win out there. She doesn't deserve your behaviour," Mum says.

He looks at Dakota. "Sorry," he says and then stomps away like a spoilt child.

I start laughing; I just can't help myself.

"I think I'd better go. Scarlett, it was great to see you, and if you stay with this handsome devil," Dakota says smiling at me, "then I will see a lot more of you. Give me a ring in the week and let's catch up."

"For sure," Scarlett says, grabbing my hand.

Dakota leaves and Scarlett turns to my parents. "Sorry for my outburst, but he really pissed me off." She looks down to the floor.

"Scarlett, someone needed to put Keaton in his place and you just did. Well done, and don't be sorry. He is always an arsehole when Dakota is around." Mum says, laughing.

"Yeah, baby. Don't worry about Keaton. He will probably get really drunk tonight. That's what usually happens when they've been around each other. Let's go. We're going to Mixology tonight."

I take her hand and help her onto my bike. Before I put the helmet on for her, I lean forward and kiss her. "You're sexy when you're angry. I might just make you mad to see you being angry." I chuckle.

"Fuck off, Hunter," she says, laughing. She sticks her tongue out at me and I take it into my mouth. I devour her. God, I want her so bad. When I pull away, I say, "I am going to fuck you hard when we get home and then we're going out." I put the helmet on her head before she can answer and climb on the bike in front of her.

She puts her arms around my waist and holds me tight, and I can feel her breathing on my back. Then she reaches down and squeezes my cock which makes it hard instantaneously. "'Til later," she says. Laughing, I start the bike and set off home.

EPILOGUE

SCARLETT

We're going to Hunter's parents' home for Sunday dinner. I know I've met them a few times, but I'm still nervous about having dinner with them. It's been six weeks since I met the James family and my life has changed so much. I practically moved in with Hunter from the moment we started dating. Neither of us wanted to be apart for long and I never seemed to go home. He has met my parents and they love him. Let's be honest though; what's not to love about him? He's gorgeous, talented, funny and he has his own business. But more than that, he is so good for me, and so good to me. I've never been looked after as much as he looks after me. He can't do enough for me and I love it.

Sunday dinner at his parents' is a really big thing. Not that it's formal, but the whole family has to be there. This is the first time an 'outsider' has been invited and I'm shitting myself.

"Hunter, do I look all right?" I ask him for the umpteenth time.

"Baby, you look gorgeous, but you know that. I've told you already. What are you panicking about? You've met my whole family lots of times. You even stood up to Keaton, which was the highlight of my life. You'll be fine. Come on. It's time to go." He leans down and kisses me. Just enough for me to be left wanting more, but knowing I won't get a release until later tonight.

"Come on then. Let's do this," I say, dragging him by the arm out of the apartment.

Y Y Y

When we climb off the bike, the nerves set in again, but I take a deep breath and pull up my big girl pants. Hunter opens the door to his parents. "Hi. I'm home," he shouts as he turns to wink at me.

We walk through into the conservatory where Zac, Keaton, and Ainsley are already sitting with their parents. I take a seat and I'm handed a glass of prosecco.

"We're just waiting for Skylar then we can have dinner," his mum, Verity asks.

The door opens and Skylar shouts, "I'm here! Where's the food?"

Everyone laughs. Skylar is the quietest of the family and the one person I haven't interacted with much. He was there for me in the hospital and I hope - if he ever needs any help - that he knows I would do anything for him.

We sit down for dinner, which is gorgeous. The banter is fun around the table.

"So, Hunter, what's going on with you this week?" his Verity asks.

"Not much. We're busy in the bar. The singles week was a huge success and we're trying to work out when to do another one and what to do next to draw the same crowds in."

"Great. What about you, Keaton?"

"I've had some down time, but I'll be back on dawn patrol soon enough. The UK Championship is in a few weeks so I'm going to be taking some time out from Mixology to concentrate on surfing for the last couple of weeks."

"That's great, Keaton. You know we're behind you every step of the way." She smiles at him.

"So is Dakota," Zac says, laughing.

"Watch it Zac," Keaton says. It's so funny how he gets when anyone talks about Dakota. He hates her with such a passion that if I didn't know him better, I'd say he was in love with her.

"Zac, what about you?" Verity asks.

"Well, my mates went back home and they keep trying to get me to go back to fighting …"

"No fucking way," Keaton and Hunter say at the same time.

"Don't worry, I'm not interested in doing that anymore. They just aren't listening to me. Other than that, I've only been in the gym and working at Mixology. A quiet week for me too. I haven't had to throw anyone out for a long time." He laughs.

"Thank God for that," Hunter says.

Verity laughs. "Ainsley, you're being quiet and spending a lot of time on your phone. What's going on with you?"

Ainsley looks like she's been caught out. Like a deer in the headlights. She stuffs her phone in her pocket.

"Erm… nothing much going on. Keeping busy with the accounts and stuff. Not much time for anything else, to be honest."

I feel sorry for Ainsley. She has four really protective brothers watching over her. Any guy that goes near her is chased off before they get within an inch of her.

"Skylar, what about you son?" Jack asks.

"Not much here either. I've been checking out some new software and some new lights, but will let you all know after I make a decision."

Skylar keeps himself to himself. I wouldn't be able to tell you what he gets up to outside of Mixology as I never see him. He doesn't come up to Hunter's apartment much and I only see him at the bar.

We're on the coffee after a heavenly dinner and even better dessert.

"Scarlett, what's been happening with you this week?" Verity asks me.

I'm shocked. I'm not family. "Me?"

She laughs. "Yes. You're here for Sunday dinner. That means we get to hear what you've been up to as well."

I feel myself blush.

I look around the table and see everyone smiling

at me. Hunter nods his head for me to go on. "Erm… well, work has been busy and I've been helping Ainsley with some of the admin at Mixology. I really enjoy it and look forward to doing more."

"Yeah, you've been a great help. Wish we could take you on full time," Ainsley says, smiling at me.

"That's not a bad idea, Ains," Hunter says, looking at his sister.

"I know. I'm clever, you know? I don't like letting any responsibility go to a stranger, but there is more and more work involved with running the bar. You're okay at helping, Hunter, but your organizational skills leave a lot to be desired. Scarlett has already shown what she is capable of doing. With her working at the law firm, she understands a lot of the jargon that I don't understand."

"Are you guys offering me a job?" I ask, surprised.

Hunter looks at Ainsley and his brothers. They all nod. "Looks like it, baby. Do you want to be a part of the Mixology team?"

He looks so sweet watching me try to make a decision in my mind. "I … I think I'd like that."

They all smile and cheer and there is another glass of prosecco that comes out of nowhere.

When we get back to Hunter's apartment, we stand on the balcony, looking out to sea. It's become our favourite spot. Hunter has his arms wrapped tight around my waist and he's holding me close. He leans down and kisses my neck. "I love you, Scarlett," he says. I hold my breath. "You've come into my life and turned it upside down, but in the best way possible. I never want to go back to my life before you came along. I floated along, just existing, but not living. Now, I'm living the dream.

"I love you too, Hunter. That night I met you led to the craziest week in my life. But I would do it all again just to meet you."

ACKNOWLEDGMENTS

There are always too many people to acknowledge and I always know that I will forget someone important. Sorry!

I try to think of one or two people who helped me with each book and I wanted to give a special shout out to Kirsty-Anne Still of Designs by Kirsty-Anne Still. She helped me with the cover. I gave her free range to do what she wanted along the 'Cocktail' theme with neon sign etc. I think she has done a marvellous job and am so happy with the whole series of covers. Thank you so much for bringing my visions to life with your amazing talent.

ABOUT THE AUTHOR

I hated English at school! Really hated it! I gave up on English Literature in fourth year because I hated writing stories; couldn't make them up to save my life. I hated writing precis and I was horrendous at grammar. Having lived in Norway when I was younger, English was my second language.

When I received my iPad six years ago I started reading on the kindle app and wrote to an author about how much I enjoyed her book. That opened up the whole facebook author world to me. I started reviewing books (ironic, right?) and then started beta reading (even more ironic) after pointing out some big mistakes in a book plot I was reviewing before release.

I realised I had a story in me, yeah I know everyone says that, but I really believed I did. Thirteen books later …. Welcome to the world of Krissy V!